From The World of Strangers and Pilgrims

Book One:

CONFLICT WITH SHADOWS

SECOND EDITION

BY:
MARK CASTLEBERRY

SECOND EDITION

ISBN: 979-8-9853947-4-0 (Paperback)
ISBN: 978-1-0881-3830-4 (E-Book)

Library of Congress Control Number: 2023910504

Any references to historical events, real people, or real places are used fictitiously. Names, characters, and places are products of the author's imagination.

Front cover image by Wonder.
Book design by Mark Castleberry.

Printed in the United States of America.

First printing edition 2019.

Strangers and Pilgrims Publishing
www.strangerspilgrims.com

TABLE OF CONTENTS

For Jennifer

And for my readers

These all died in faith, not having received the promises, but having seen them afar off, and were persuaded of *them*, and embraced *them*, and confessed that they were strangers and pilgrims on the earth.
- Hebrews 11:13 KJV

Now faith is the substance of things hoped for, the evidence of things not seen. -Hebrews 11:1 KJV

CHAPTER ONE
Six Years Before War

With his wrists in cuffs and his legs in shackles, Jonah sat in the back of the prison transport heading to Black Star, the Alliance secret dark prison. The facility had been constructed for people like himself, far among hidden stars. Because he had been labeled a terrorist Jonah was not given a trial, or any chance to prove otherwise. Jonah never considered himself a terrorist. An assassin for hire, perhaps, better fit the description of his line of work. How exactly he got is his current situation, he wasn't sure. One thing he knew for sure, though, was that he had to have been set up.

Jonah was very good at his chosen trade; so perfect in fact, that he could have never gotten himself captured on his own. No one in galactic society knew his face. The only description that had ever gotten out to the Locals was the color of his eyes. "They was shiny blue, so light that they looked like glass," were the exact words used. For a long time, he had been on the Alliance's most wanted list, and that was classified of course.

His mind switched to just who could have set him up. He had gotten captured on Tiere, the capital world of the Alliance. Simon Kohl, one of his few trusted informants, was on Tiere. He was a short, seedy-looking man who believed himself to be one of the intellectual elite. Jonah could see Simon ratting him out to someone for fear of his own life, but Simon couldn't set him up alone. However, he was the only lead so far that he had.

Jonah's target had been the Senator of Chotis. He was not a high priority target, so the security for him was minimal. It was going to be an easy job. Thinking about it now, it had been too easy.

He had lined up the sights on the sniper rifle to the head of the Senator making his way out of the Alliance Senatorial Building. There would be plenty of time to get away when the job was finished. Before the Senator disappeared around the corner, he pulled the trigger, and the Senator fell. It had been smooth and quiet. As he began dismantling the rifle, the door of the room he occupied burst open, and the Locals came through the door, guns out of holsters and pointed at him, followed by an Alliance Agent.

The Agent's name was Jon Vega, and Jonas knew him. He knew him because this same Jon Vega had been after him for nearly two years now. Now he seemed to have him. "You finally caught me, Vega. Someone had to have turned me in," he said to him.

Jon Vega stood there and watched as the prisoner was handcuffed. Jon replied, "It doesn't matter; you're not going to be free anymore in this lifetime."

Now he was being transported to Black Star. He placed his right hand inside his left, took his thumb, and started digging hard at his wrist. Soon drops of blood began seeping out. Jonah was not going to be going to this secret prison. Soon a slit formed in his wrist just above the arteries, and he used his thumb to slide out the hidden skeleton key he had stored there many years ago. Quietly he flipped on the key's power and placed it close to the cuffs' computer, and it searched for the cuffs' combination. A few moments later, the cuffs snapped open, and Jonah did the same to the shackles.

The single guard sitting across from him with the rifle had started falling asleep. The shackles had been attached to the flooring of the shuttle but had fallen away, so he quickly jumped at the snoozing guard, his elbow crushing the man's neck. The guard gave an uppercut to him, knocking him back. As Jonah fell, he grabbed the pistol from the guard's side holster and shot the guard in the face before the guard could react again.

The guard fell back against the hull, then slumped over dead.

As Jonah stood up, he heard the announcement over the speaker. "Coming back into real space now. Twenty minutes to Black Star docking. Get the prisoner ready, Case. He is nearly out of our hands."

Jonah smiled to himself. He made his way to the pilot's cockpit and slid open the door. Out of the viewport, Jonah saw Black Star in the distance. The co-pilot looked up, and before he could say anything, Jonah shot him in the neck. The pilot had time to switch on the distress signal, just before he died. Jonah pulled the pilot from his seat and took over. Soon the transport shuttle had turned around and vanished back into hyperspace.

Jon Vega was eating lunch in a corner cafe on the busy streets of Sandal, the capital city of Tiere. His boss, Commander Dorman slid, into the chair across from him. "Jonah never made it to prison," he stated, trying to get a reaction out of him.

There was no reaction from him at all. He just looked back over his coffee cup. "How far did he get in that shuttle?" Jon had walked Jonah to the shuttle himself and watched it lift off.

"They found the shuttle on the Synoa mining facility, abandoned. Apparently, he took a job on one of the carriers heading toward the seven moons of Gin Kojoda. That is all we know."

"How did he get it through the tunnel and past the Synoa station?"

Commander Dorman just looked at him. "He was on a Republic shuttle. The codes were on the computer. His escape had not yet been known."

"You think he is coming back here?" Jon asked him.

Dorman nodded. "Very possible." He stood back up. "I'd watch your back. He might be after you for catching him."

I don't think so, Jon thought as the Commander walked away. He knew where Jonah might go.

Erik Bond's office was a bit run down, located in a part of the city that was considered shabby, and that was known for its criminal morals. There were, however, many honest people living in this sector of Necros. The rest of the city was thriving as this sector continued to fall into destitution. This was fine for the business Erik Bond was doing.

He ran an employment service of sorts. He found jobs for those who could not get jobs by any other means. Like a hit-man.

A man walked in, closed the door, and walked up to Erik, who was sitting behind the desk. "What can I do for you, sir?" Erik asked, smiling.

"Do you know a man named Simon Kohl?"

Erik looked him over. "You a Local?" he asked, referring to the police.

The man shook his head. "No, he was a friend?"

"Then what do you want from me?"

The man sat down in one of the cheap chairs in front of the desk. "You hired him to find someone to kill the Chotis Senator. I want to know if this was your job, or if someone came to you with the job?"

Erik was taken aback. "Are you sure you're not a Local?"

"I'm not a cop," replied the man. "I'm the one who did the job."

After a few moments, Erik let out a sigh of relief. This man was someone in his world. "And you want more money," he finally replied.

"I want to know who gave you the job."

"My clients don't like to be revealed; its what keeps me alive, and in business."

The man pulled out a knife, its blade stained with dried blood. "Simon gave me your name with his dying breath, because he, too, didn't give his clients' names out."

It only took a second for Erik to change his mind. "I only met with a woman, called herself Soshiana. She was stunning, long black hair. She was thin, but strong as a bull." Erik paused and stared at the man, hoping to see some sign of acceptance. There was none.

Erik continued. "She dressed nice, and she came to me, just not here. It was over at Garden Park in the central sector of Necros. She gave me the details there. She never said if she worked for anyone. I assumed it was her job. She paid in cash."

The man just stared at him. "Is that the only name she gave you?"

"Yes," Erik nodded. "And there was something odd about her. No emotion, never even smiled, everything straight up."

The man seemed to think about it. Then he picked up the knife, stood up, and put it away. "Thank you, Mr. Bond. And if you ever have a job, look me up."

Erik stood up, being cordial. "I don't know your name, sir."

"Jonah."

"Just Jonah?"

"Just Jonah," the man confirmed. "Like, just Soshiana."

Jon Vega stood in the office of Simon Kohl. The man's body was slumped against the wall with his head leaning back, and his eyes were open but dead. The Tiere Local Agent, Ben Gettel, stood up from the body and turned toward Jon.

"Looks like a single stab wound in the gut," he told him. "Are we sure this was Jonah?"

Jon looked around, nodding. "Yea, I'm almost certain.

It's where the trail led. We need to look around to see if we can find any evidence of where he might have gone next."

Ben began rummaging through the filing cabinets, and Jon sat down behind the desk and looked around. The top of the desk had been cleaned off, although it seemed as if several of the papers had been tossed onto the floor. He picked them up and looked at them. Nothing. Just adverts and junk mail. He then opened the top desk drawer and found more papers, a bit of cash, and a file folder.

The papers were nothing, just more junk and bills. The folder was another matter. It held jobs he had been given to give to Jonah. The file folder contained all of Jonah's appointments, and there were many.

"I think I found what we need," he said to Ben, who turned around and walked up to the desk. "When we catch him again, we'll have more to charge him with."

"Is all that about Jonah?"

After a moment, Jon found what he was looking for. "Jonah was caught assassinating the Chotis Senator, wasn't he?"

"Yea."

"This job came from a man from Chotis," Jon said.

"From one Erik Bond." He turned to Ben. "Who's the Agent on Chotis?"

Ben smiled. "Her name is Saffron Baye."

Jon looked up at him and saw the smile. He used to date Saffron many years ago before he became an Alliance Agent. They were together when he had had Ben's job here on Tiere, as a Local Agent. "When did she get promoted?"

"Four years ago. Ray retired," Ben told him. "She was his second."

Jon let out a sigh. "Well, contact her for me, and tell her to expect me."

The Tiere Agent stood straight up. "It must not have ended well between you two."

"It was a mutual breakup," Jon told him. "Career choices and such." After a few moments, Jon stood up, taking the folder. "Just let her know I'm on my way."

"Sure thing," Ben replied.

Three days later Jon arrived in the Local Agent office in Angora, the capitol city of Chotis. He saw Saffron sitting behind her desk. Her red hair was no longer down her back but was now cut just above her shoulders, but Jon noticed her bright blue eyes still shone when she smiled.

"Well, well, if it isn't my old beau, Jon Vega," she said before anything could come out of his mouth. Saffron continued, "Fancy seeing you here after you broke my heart."

Jon closed the door, finally, and walked on inside. "As I remember it, the breakup was mutual."

Saffron smiled. "You broke up with me so you could become an Alliance Agent. Besides, if you hadn't, I probably would be sitting in a cottage somewhere worrying about your health or something."

It finally occurred to him it was a joke. "Ben set this up?"

She nodded and laughed a little. "Yea. He told me he picked on you a bit."

Relieved, Jon sat down across from her. Then she sat up straighter and spoke. "So I hear you tracked the infamous Jonah here."

"Yea, I believe so. I think he came to see a man named Erik Bond, who issued the job for the Chotis Senator assassination."

Saffron handed him a card she had written up for him. "And I found him. He has an office in the city of Necros, north of here. We can be there in a couple of hours."

"The sooner, the better," Jon said. "The last man he visited ended up with a knife wound in the stomach."

Both stood up, and Jon let her lead the way out the door. "I have an aircar waiting outside."

Two and a half hours later Jon and Saffron walked into the office of Erik Bond. Erik was surprised when they showed him their identifications. "What can I do for the Alliance Agent Corp?"

Jon took out the folder he had taken from Simon Kohl's office. He took out the paper about the Chotis Senator and slapped it down on Erik's desk. "You hired Simon Kohl to get someone to kill the Chotis Senator."

Erik was surprised. Beads of sweat started to form on his forehead and neck.

'Oh no," he thought to himself. He glanced at the paper, and he knew they knew. "It was only a job."

"Your job is to hire criminals to kill decent people." Both Saffron's voice and posture showed anger.

Jon tapped her shoulder, trying to calm her down. "So you admit this was your job?" he asked calmly.

Erik just nodded, shamefully. There wasn't much else he could do.

"Now I have another question," he continued. "Has Jonah come to visit you?"

Suddenly, he remembered the knife Jonah had pulled out in front of him. He didn't want to see it again. Erik thought about it for a minute before answering the question. This would be the first time he had ever sold anyone out. He remembered what he told Jonah. It would be the second time.

"He was here," he finally said. "He wanted to know who gave me the job."

"Did you tell him?"

"I told him that a woman calling herself Soshiana found me in Garden Park."

Soshiana worked for a man known throughout the galaxy as the Godfather of the Galaxy, Thermonte Electrik, and was a name known to Jon. But Soshiana was no ordinary woman. She was a BioTek, the only one known to exist still. BioTek production had been outlawed decades ago. It seemed that the process of combining technology with flesh, even near-death flesh, made those who were operated on to go mad, killing others or themselves.

But this Soshiana was one of a kind. One, she was strictly loyal to Thermonte, and no one else. Two, the problem with the other Biotek experiments seemed to have been fixed. He had always wondered who had done the job on her.

Jon turned to Saffron. "I know where to go now." He picked up the paper from Erik's desk and placed it back in the folder. "You want to come?" he asked her.

"Wouldn't miss it for the world," she answered, then walked to the door and motioned for the Locals to enter before turning back to Erik. "Erik Bond, you are under arrest for conspiracy in the death of Senator Lawler of Chotis, and anything else we can find."

The Locals took Erik into custody and cuffed his hands behind his back before taking him out the door. "Contact the Agency in Angora, and have him transported to the prison there. I will deal with him when I get back."

"Yes, Ma'am," one of the Locals replied.

Jon looked at her. "Not going to let the Locals take care of it?"

"You have been away from the Local Agency. Death of a senator is Planetary jurisdiction. "

It took two days from when Jonah left Erik's office to find Soshiana. Or, in other words, Soshiana found Jonah. He was in Garden Park when she came up to him.

"You're the man they call Jonah," she just stated.

"And who are you?"

"I'm Soshiana," she replied, holding her hand out for a greeting.

Jonah stood up from the park bench he was sitting on. "You set me up," he said in anger.

"No, I did not. But my employer did. And I am here to take you to him."

"Then let us go," he answered.

Soshiana stood there, arm outstretched, her hand opened. "Please be cordial first, Jonah. Shake my hand."

Jonah just looked at her. This woman was strange. He finally reached out and shook her hand. "DNA scan," he realized. She smiled and said, "Follow me; it's time to meet my employer."

They took a Skimmer into the mountains just east of Necros. There was a huge house built into the side of a mountain, overlooking a lake. Once they set down, Jonah followed her into the house. The foyer was large, with dark hardwood floors. It was minimalistic and lit very dimly. He saw a painting of an older lady on one of the walls.

She pointed to a closed door on the side. "That is the

den. He is in there waiting for you." Then she turned to go further into the house.

"Where are you going?" he asked her.

"I have other things to do," she replied, walking away.

Once she was out of his sight, Jonah reached down from his boot and removed the knife he had used against Simon. He slowly made his way to the door, waiting to be attacked, but no one struck. He opened the door and walked in.

Sitting on the sofa on the far side of the room was a big man, overweight by the looks of him. He had a mustache and neatly trimmed goatee naturally colored to cover up any grey. He had a drink in his hand, and he waved it around as he spoke. "It's about time you showed up, Jonah. I have always wanted to meet the great secret assassin."

Jonah gripped the knife in his fist. "So you set me up to go to prison," he said harshly.

"I knew you would escape and find me," Thermonte told him. "I had to find out just how good you were."

"What are you talking about?"

The fat man took a drink. "I want to offer you a job, Jonah. You would become so rich, and I can guarantee that the entire galaxy would believe you to be dead. But you would be rich and alive."

Jonah just shook it off. "I'm already rich. I have millions in cash."

"Not anymore, my friend," the Godfather replied. "All of that was seized when they captured you."

"Because you sold me out."

"Ehh," was the reply. "Minor detail. I will replace all that just for you to sign up working for me." He took another drink.

Jonah didn't say a word. He just thought about it. There was something he needed to know. "So why did you set me up?"

"As I said before, I knew you would escape. I wanted to see just how good you are, and you are good," Thermonte said to him. "Escaping right before incarceration, that was excellent work."

"So it was a test?"

Thermonte nodded in agreement. "Yea, that is a good way to put it."

"Do you do this to all your employees?"

"Just the outstanding ones." After a moment's pause and a drink large enough to finish the liquid, he asked, "So, are you in?"

"I don't know," was the reply. Jonah was trying his

best to think this through.

"Well, you had better hurry and decide." Thermonte stood up and made his way to the wet bar to his right and walked behind it. "The Alliance Agency Corp are on their way here. In fact, they are almost here."

Jonah looked around almost frantically, instinctively. "Are you setting me up again?"

"Of course not. The Locals are looking for you. You're an escaped criminal, and they are following your trail. Simple as that."

Jonah calmed himself down, though he was still holding the knife, waiting for a fight. "How would you fix it, so they think I'm dead, without killing me?"

Thermonte poured himself another drink while explaining. "I have a facility out beyond galactic civilization. Your face would be changed, your fingerprints and your DNA would be hidden. The entire process takes about nine months, and then you would be given a new name and a new outlook on life."

There was a beep, and Thermonte turned on a nearby monitor. "You better hurry and decide. The Locals are about to land."

What choice did he have? Jonah agreed to join, and Thermonte gave Soshiana the go-ahead. She led Jonah from the room, which would be the last time anyone would see him.

Thermonte Electrik finished his second drink, and as he poured himself another, Jon Vega and Saffron Baye were led into the room by one of the Godfather's associates, followed by Locals. "Nice to see you again, Agent Vega. Welcome to my humble home."

"Not so humble by my standards," Jon replied. "I think you know why we are here."

"Of course," Thermonte replied, walking out from behind the wet bar. "It's about that escaped convict. He was here. And to protect me, my men shot and killed him."

He nodded to one of his men. They went out and brought in a body and laid it on the floor. Jon knelt beside the body and examined it. It looked as if his face had been shot up with a Blast Shot, a projectile weapon. "We sure this is him?" Jon asked. "His face is gone."

Saffron handed him a DNA scanner. Jon took it and touched the face and waited for the result. It came out positive. "It's him," Jon said, still somewhat wary of the result. "It's Jonah."

Then he stood up and looked back at Thermonte. "So you hired him to kill the Chotis Senator, and then killed off the assassin?"

"Now, why would I do that? Senator Lawler and I were great friends. We appeared together several times at public events."

Saffron grinned. "A criminal and senator together."

"Just because I am rich, doesn't make me a criminal, Agent Baye. And unfounded accusations will get the Agency into trouble," Thermonte said seriously. "Now I would hope you would take this body and leave."

Jon knew he was right. His name was not on any paperwork he had gathered on the Senator's murder, and neither was Soshiana's. Thermonte Electrik's tracks were covered well. They all knew he was a criminal, but without proof, nothing could be done. And everyone here would say it was self-defense.

He ordered the Locals to take the body away. But before he left, he spoke once more to the fat man. "Don't leave anytime soon, Mr. Electrik. We still need to fill out a report for the records."

Thermonte nodded. "Sure thing, Agent."

Twelve hours later, Jonah was led to a secret landing port hidden in the mountains. Soshiana watched him board, and the ship took off for the facility far out beyond civilized space. To the galaxy, Jonah the assassin was dead, and the man, Thermonte Electrik, would be considered a hero.

CHAPTER TWO
Attacking The Peace

The peaceful world of Serenity hung in the blackness of space alone. It didn't even have a moon. Its location was unclaimed by both the Republic and the Union Federation governments, but the peoples of both were welcome. The cold war between the two factions still lingered on since the unitary split, which took place nearly three decades ago. Both galactic factions spied on one another, kept tabs on one another to stay ahead of their enemy. There was an agreement to locate worlds where peace between the two peoples could be maintained, and neutrality was the law there. Serenity was not the only world unclaimed by both factions, another was the world of Bel Terra, which was located on the far side of known space. It was protected by both factions but was abandoned long, long ago due to over-population and environmental issues.

However, it was Serenity that an unknown enemy had decided to attack. It was easy and quick. The attacking battleship looked as if it had three saucers lined together, the front smaller than the others connecting to one another, with the rear section holding the engines. Small towers and small domes covered the top, and smaller black domes were scattered beneath, and it was black. Black as the darkness of space itself. Only the lights that surrounded the ship told you it was there. The front end lit up, and many smaller vessels, fighters, swarmed out like ants from a mound. They looked like little triangles, cockpit in the front, guns on the bottom, fins on top.

From the surface of the planet, it seemed to block out the system's sun, and the people there stopped and looked upward at the coming storm. When the giant shadow moved away from the light, it was replaced by the tiny specks of the fighters coming in, growing larger. Behind the smaller fighters came larger ships, like insects with V-shaped wings heading down toward the city streets of Damascus, the capital city. The fighters flew in firing at the people, sending small missiles at the buildings, destroying them and scattering rubble all around.

Many of the people died, and the rest of them ran hiding from the shots. The shuttles landed and deposited black-clad troops to round up Damascus' citizens. More died. Some of the people fought back with whatever they could get ahold of.

From a nearby landing port, soldiers on furlough had grabbed weapons which were left on their own Republic shuttles and began a whole new battle on the ground. They met up with the local security, and finally, they were making headway. A lot of the attackers fell, and many of the soldiers and Locals fell. Many of them, however, were slowly driven back into local buildings.

On board the Republic shuttle, two communications operators were trying to get a message to the Republic. They had just reached a Republic battleship when an enemy missile struck the landing port and destroying it completely collapsing onto the shuttle.

This attack of Serenity didn't last long, for it was an easy target, even with the problem with the soldiers. The attacking fighters retreated back into the ship, then two more enemy battleships appeared, and from one of them, another enemy shuttle landed near the capitol building. Most of the citizens had all been rounded up, some were still hiding out, and the soldiers were trapped in surrounding buildings. A tall, broad-shouldered man walked out in a proud strut followed by more black-clad troops and a blond-haired man. The tall man was an older man, with thin grey hair and a scar on his lip running down to his chin.

Troopers led a man from the capitol building and stood him in front of the newcomers. It was Senator Clay, Serenity's leader, chosen by both the Republic and Federation. The man said, "I am Admiral Gedor. Do you have communications to both the Republic and the Federation?"

Frightened, Senator Clay nodded that he had. "Yes," he said feebly.

"Take me there now."

Senator Clay led the way back into the building followed by Admiral Gedor and his troopers.

The Comm Officer who was talking to the soldiers on Serenity had heard the explosion of the port, and the silence that followed alerted him to send a message to the Commander of the battleship Deliverer, Commander Lawler. "Sir, there seems to be a problem on the surface of Serenity."

"What kind of problem?"

"There was an explosion and then silence on their end."

"Explosion?" There was a surprise in his voice. He thought a moment. "Get me General Brande."

General Thomas Brande was sitting in a staff meeting when the call came through. His private secretary came through the door silently and handed the note to him and stood to wait for an answer. The other five members stopped talking and waited patiently. Brande looked around the room and made the decision. "Put the call through in here and put it on the speaker." To the others, he said, "You might want to hear this."

The speaker snapped on, and Brande told Commander Lawler to deliver the message. Lawler's voice came on. "We had a call from soldiers on furlough on Serenity. Specifically in Damascus. Here is the message we got."

The voice was from the soldier in the spaceport in Damascus. "This is Unit 372 on Serenity, can anyone read me."

"This is Republic battleship Deliverer," was the reply from Comm Officer.

"Deliverer, We are under att...", then came the explosion and the silence.

Sitting in the meeting was President Norris, the official leader of the Republic. He was the first to speak out. "You don't think the Federation would attack Serenity without provocation?"

Just then Brande's private secretary came back in. This time he was speaking to President Norris. "Sir, Prime Minister Lamet is on the line, and he's not happy."

"Put him on speaker, soldier," replied the President. "Let's hear what he has to say."

The speaker hummed to life again, and the angry voice of the Prime Minister spoke. "Just what is the Republic up doing attacking Serenity. Federation citizens were killed and this could start a war."

"Hold on, Prime Minister, we just got the news of the attack ourselves," the President interrupted.

Lamet continued to speak. "Our fleet is prepared to defend our borders and we're sending a battle group to Serenity to destroy your fleet."

President Norris interrupted him again. The Prime Minister was a passionate man when it came to the Federation. He always had been. "It is not us, Prime Minister. The Republic is not responsible for this attack.

Republic citizens died also."

There was finally silence on the Prime Minister's end. Those in the staff meeting held their breath, waiting. Then it came.

"President Norris," the Prime Minister said, "I think we need to have a conference in person."

"Where do you suggest Prime Minister Lamet?"

After a few moments, The Prime Minister said, "How about Synoa Station? It was built to be neutral."

President Norris looked around at the others in the room. "Very well. And may I suggest we each send a re-con team to Serenity and bring the results with us."

"Yes, yes, excellent idea," replied PM Lamet. "I will be on board our command ship the Fiat."

"I will be on the Independence."

After other arrangements had been and the two leaders had agreed to them, and the communications between them had been cut off, President Norris turned to the General. "You're with me, and bring one of your top agents. And get Admiral Clark ready on the Independence."

Admiral Gedor was back on the bridge of his

command ship, as the blond man approached. "The link-up is made, Admiral. When will you make the announcement?"

Gedor stared out the viewport at the planet below. "We must wait for the right time."

"But sir..."

"Sir," the radar officer interrupted. "We have a small craft entering the system."

"How close are they coming?" Gedor asked.

"Not too close, but they're scanning the system, specifically Serenity and us."

The blond man moved closer. "What is this?"

"Sir, another small ship has entered the system. This one is moving closer."

"They'll see us," the blond man said.

Admiral Gedor said. "Settle yourself, Chelli. It's all part of the plan. Just be prepared if their battleships get through. We're not ready for a fight yet."

The blond man scowled. He hated when Admiral Gedor called him by his surname. His was Bjorn Chelli. He was a one-time rogue mercenary working for the highest bidder. Now he worked for the Bathshe. Not for Admiral Gedor. "This is not the plan, Admiral. You are starting a war here."

"I'm testing their defenses, Chelli." There was detest in his voice. "This is the plan. Your job is to obey."

Bjorn Chelli knew what he had to do. Gedor was power-hungry, he enjoyed fighting way too much. This was not going to end well for him. But Pan had told them both the plan. Bjorn would have to do what he needed to do to get the job done. "May I be dismissed, sir?"

Gedor's tension had left his voice, and it was calm. He was in control again. "Of course."

Bjorn turned and walked off the bridge and found his own personal team waiting for him in the docking bay. They stood before a ship, his own ship he had used so many years ago. The starship he used when he was recruited for this job, which was now his life.

"Well?" asked his first in command. "What's the deal?"

"We head out before he jumps."

The two shuttle crafts slowly moved toward the enemy, scanning and getting the information. Jon Vega was in one of the shuttles, he didn't know who was in the other. He was sure he would find out later. The design was strange, but the weapons seemed to be created by mankind. That might be true with Gedor seemingly being in charge.

The comm buzzed on his panel, and he answered. It was the other shuttle. "This is Nicolea Dan of the Federation to the Republic shuttle. Are you there?"

"This is Jon Vega of the Republic. I thought we weren't supposed to communicate with one another."

"Yea, well, I tend to go with my gut in 'not supposed to' situations. " His accent was not quite as thick as Jon would have expected.

Jon smiled. "Understood. So what's up?"

"Are you seeing what I'm seeing? Something is weird about this. Where has Admiral Gedor been all this time? We figured he was dead or something."

"Your guess is as good as mine." Then something on the scanner caught his attention. "Look at that dome on the front of the ship. It's opening up."

Both of them watched as what looked to be a giant laser cannon projected itself out and fired a large projectile toward Serenity. Fear rose up in both of them, and all they could do was watch. They both knew what it was. The missile hit the planet below, wiping out the city of Damascus and its surrounding areas. Jon felt like he was going to be sick. Then something even more horrifying happened. More ships came into view, and when it was over with, there were twelve in all. Six of them split from the fleet and headed toward Federation space, disappearing in hyperspace. The other six, however, moved pass the burning world of Serenity and jumped deeper into Republic space.

Jon sat in silence for a long time after. Then the comm buzzed again. "I guess we had better report this. I'll see you at Synoa Station." The Federation shuttle made its jump, and soon after Jon followed. A small freighter was all that was left in the space above Serenity, and the pilot had named it Bird Of Prey back when he was a bounty hunter. Bjorn still had his original team, and they had all signed up to work for this Pan. Gedor was going off script, and he realized that the real mission may not get finished because of his self seeking pride.

The Synoa system was made up mostly of asteroids. There was a mining facility in its center used to mine lithium from the asteroids use as fuel in all sorts of ships. They supplied both factions and remained neutral in the cold war between the two governments. It was one of only a few free agents agreed upon in the known galaxy.

On the outskirts on the field sat a massive space station, hanging like a spider from its web.

The station was like other space station, tubular like in design with large communication wings extending our the front sides. The communication extensions stretching out toward the asteroid field kept in touch with the mining station within, and could operate the tunneling process which would let one through the field. Shuttles could land in the small docking bay located beneath the station, with larger ships standing patrol several clicks away in order to let transport ships in and out of the mining facility. It was here that the two leaders of the factions met. It was once used as an armistice station during the Border Wars, now seemed to be used as a joint base to help decide what to do about this new enemy that threatened both of them.

Jon walked into the command center, where the leaders were waiting. Nicolea was already there. He was tall, blond, not bad looking, and had a scar across the bridge of his nose. Jon figured he had seen some action.

"Jon, " President Norris spoke. "The Federation agent, Nicolea Dan," he said it slowly making sure he said it correctly. The blond agent nodded. Norris continued, "has been telling us what happened at

Serenity. Can you confirm his story?"

"If his story has to do with Serenity's destruction and the ships, then yes." The two leaders looked at one another, as did the other council members and security in the room. "Six of those battleships moved deeper into our space, and six moved deeper into Federation space. They're giving us two fronts to work with."

The Union Federation Prime Minister looked toward his own agent. "Do you have any idea where the first fleet was headed into Federation space?"

Jon thought that his accent was much more of what he thought it should be. Much thicker. Then Nicolea answered, "I'm not sure, but the direction looked to be headed toward Vandemic, sir".

The Prime Minister leaned back and spoke to one of his advisers. "Contact Admiral Astarte. Tell him to investigate Vandemic now." The adviser nodded and began his task.

President Norris turned toward Jon. "What about the other fleet?"

"Just moving deeper the way they did, I would suspect Jasper. But I wouldn't rule out Tiere."

Norris then spoke to Commander Dorman. "Send General Brande to Jasper and contact Grand Admiral

Shepherd, and get him to Tiere with his fleet. "

"Yes, Sir." the Commander replied and moved toward the other end of the console.

Then to Lamet, Norris asked, "What would be the purpose of dividing their fleet like they did?"

In a slightly arrogant way, PM Lamet spoke. "Perhaps they think their battleships are stronger and better equipped than ours. Well, they haven't seen Federation warships in action."

"Perhaps they want to make sure we don't work together," Norris replied.

Jon interrupted, "We need to find out." Everyone agreed. "May I see the footage again?"

Norris looked at Lamet, then told Commander Dorman to play the video. The room was quiet as the video played. It was on a screen sitting between the two communication consoles. Out beyond was the view of the stars and space. When it had stopped, Jon said the first words.

"It took two minutes three seconds to open the dome and extend the cannon." President Norris shrugged, and the others seemed to agree with the confusion. Jon just continued, "It means we have a chance to at least stop the planetary destruction. We have that much time to take out the cannons once they are activated."

"Okay," Norris agreed, "But how do we achieve this?"

Nicolea spoke up then. "We test them. The first battle, we use what we have. Then we move on from there, and try something bigger and better."

"Many worlds could be destroyed by then," answered Dorman. "People would be slaughtered. You saw that footage."

"Then we need to find out something about those ships," Jon chimed in. "We need to get on board one of those."

The room was quiet then as eyes darted from one to another. Then, President Norris' eyes landed on Prime Minister Lamet's eyes, and both nodded. "You are right, Mister President," the PM said. "I can see why he is your top Agent."

The President looked back up at Jon. "We sent a probe to assess the damage on Serenity. Outside the destruction zone, they found a small camp just north. It's a military type camp. You should be able to infiltrate and get what you need to get on board one of the Bathshe ships. "

Jon looked almost stunned. Then he smiled and looked at Nicolea. "Would you mind if I took Agent

Dan with me?"

PM Lament shrugged expectedly. He looked at Nicolea. "Are you up for this mission?"

Nicolea nodded. "Of course Prime Minister."

"Then he is all yours," he said to Jon. But he is not an agent. He is a Federation Protectorate. We call them Protectors."

Jon looked over at his counterpart. "Are you ready, Protector Dan?"

"I am."

"Then let's get going. There is a stealth ship in the docking bay."

Nicolea followed Jon out the door. When they were gone, Norris turned to Commander Dorman. "Call in the rest of the team. Send them to Shepherd on the Valiance. We are going to need good fighters out there."

CHAPTER THREE
Battlefields

On the outer rim of the Cathian System, a single Bathshe battleship appeared, moving closer to the world of Cathia. A desert planet with sparse greenery watered by the occasional underground spring, it had nothing really to boast, but it was known for its uncultivated and almost primitive culture with a laid back government. The government did like to know when the brass was, though and kept a security satellite to that end.

So it was a surprise when the satellite indicated the unknown ship heading their way. Captain Braums, the commander over the wild world, decided at that moment to contact his superior because the ship matched the description they were given from them.

This continued on up the ladder until it came to President Norris on Synoa Station.

Norris was on the comm talking to Grand Admiral Shepherd. "Has the team arrived yet?" The admiral confirmed that they had. "Get over to Cathia, there is another invasion there."

The comm went blank, and he turned to see the PM on the other side of the room. Seems he was having problems of his own, Norris thought.

Jon and Nicolea had just entered the Serenity planetary atmosphere in a stealth frigate class ship, a special unit created by Ikon shipyards, under the radar of the Federation. Ikon had a lot of secrets. This information never concerned either one of the two men. They weren't stupid to the fact of it, it just wasn't their job.

They flew slowly in the upper atmosphere scanning for the encampment, using the information from the probe. It didn't take long to find it, located about two miles north of the blackened terrain, which came back as radioactive. But it was contained radioactivity, not expanding beyond that which was actually burned.

The encampment was located in a forest area within the unusually large green-barked trees. Jon landed the frigate about a mile away from a camp in a small clearing to the east. Both men were in camouflage fatigues and carried full military gear, including XL-9 light rifles each, both carrying basic handheld sidearms, and Nicolea carried the Bolt sniper rifle, and a bag full of explosives. They were ready for anything, hopefully.

They left the ship and moved slowly west toward the camp. They moved with ease, not talking. Each had earpieces to speak to the other in case if they were separated. The scanners on the rifles led the way. When they got close, they found some thick brush to duck behind and crawled under peeping out the bottom. Jon took out his field glasses and started to look around.

"Well, there they are. Dressed in dark grey, setting up some kind of system. It's strange looking."

"What about those buildings in there?" Nicolea asked. The buildings were obviously portable. "Can you read those doors?"

"Naa," Jon replied. "It's just a single strange symbol, different on each one." A moment later, he saw something that turned his face pale. "You should see this. I think I see a real Bathshe."

Nicolea was carrying the sniper rifle. He swung it around his back and into position, looking through the scope. "Where are you looking?"

"Walking out from between the two tall buildings. A little west."

The scope of the sniper moved until Nicolea could see what Jon was talking about. "Giants." Silence for a moment. "At least nine, ten feet tall. What are they carrying?"

"Looks like some sort of crude weaponry."

Nicolea scoped in closer. "Ancient more like. Giants carrying giant axes and spears."

"Well, at least they don't look ancient. They sure are clothed and ugly. And look at their eyes."

Nicolea scoped up and couldn't believe it. They had to be alien. "There is no color, but yet they can see."

Jon nodded. "And by the looks of it, they are working together."

"You think the giants are there for security?"

"Partially." He continued to look around. He noted they all had three fingers and a small protruding thumb. We need to find out what it is they are building. How good a shot are you with that thing?"

Nicolea smiled. "I've done my time with one. What do you have planned?"

Jon looked at him. "I need you to cover me. I'll sneak

around back, check out the first building, and find what I can find." He looked through the field glasses again. "You think one of those sniper blasts could take out one of those giants?"

"You get caught, we get to find out."

Jon removed most of his equipment. He took a small bag of explosive charges and his rifle and started to move toward the back of the building, the long way; around the outer perimeter of the camp.

"Lord of Light, help us." Nicolea murmured under his breath.

Grand Admiral Shepherd's fleet was made up of six destroyer class battlecruisers, three dreadnoughts, two battleships, and a single large troop carrier. Twelve ships in all. However, only two ships came to intercept the Bathshe heading toward Cathia. The Valiance and the dreadnought Portman, commanded by Commander Gordon. When they jumped into real space, they were between the planet and the Bathshe.

Quickly, small junky-looking ships came out from the belly of the main battleship and headed toward them. Shepherd gave the command for the Ikon fighters to defend.   "Those are some ugly looking fighters," Shepherd remarked.   He stood on the bridge of the Valiance and watched everything unfold. Next to him stood the agents; Ben Gettel the agent on Tiere, Saffron Baye the agent on Chotis, Gillian Lyn, the agent on Satris, Kade Poe the agent on Del Argo, and Charlie Dole, the agent on Jasper.

"You guys ready for this?" he asked them.

"We're ready," replied Ben Gettel.

"You know the assignment?"

"Yes, sir."

Shepherd nodded.   "Then get everyone to their fighters."

The Bathshe junk fighters swarmed in a tight formation, like insects ready to sting their prey. The Ikon fighters had to split apart and then wrap around back to defend the ships. They formed into their Lead and Wingman and headed straight for the swarm, firing as they came closer.   Multiple hits and multiple explosions of fire and blue gas broke up the swarm, and the Ikons were able to pick and chose their targets.

That was the moment the five light fighters containing the agents exited the Valiance and swooped back around the long way away from the battle and back around toward the Bathshe battleship. As they came closer, the warship began to fire on them; and a new swarm came out and started straight for them.

Over their headset, they heard Ben's voice. "Guys, we are in trouble. Valiance, do you hear me?"

Dreadnoughts were large rectangular shaped ships, more prominent in the back and extended wider than rest of the vessel. There were twelve levels in the ship, the lowest level was massive and contained the docking bay hold. The front looked like a fist, much smaller than the rear and it held the bridge. It could be accessed by the tenth level. Levels seven through twelve extended forward, then the bridge extended from there. Two hundred large cannon pods covered the ship each holding a single live man or woman pulling the trigger.

"We got you covered," came Shepherd's voice. "The Portman is moving around and releasing the rest of their fighters to help out. We're moving to intercept the home ship. Just get ready to take out that gun when it comes out."

The Valiance moved to fire their heavy cannons at the enemy battleship. The Bathshe fired back. The assignment had become a full-blown battle, More Ikon fighters were released from the Portman and split the belly of the new swarm easily. The Portman moved behind the Bathshe ship and began firing weapons at the engines. However, their shields were stronger than expected and the Portman made slow progress.

With the second swarm broken up, Ben called his people to follow, but keep their eyes open. "We're moving in under the belly of the beast, so keep those cannons away from us," he called to Shepherd.

"We have several harbingers coming our way guys coming starboard," announced Saffron. "I'm heading out to intercept, who's with me?"

"I'm right behind you." came Charlie's voice.

"They're called harbingers, now," Gillian said.

"Those things look horrible and scare me out of my skin."

"Alright guys, Gillian, you take first shot, then go help out with the incoming, Kade you're next, then Saffron your turn. I'll be right behind you."

Charlie said, "What about me?"

"You're the best at dogfights," replied Ben. "You bring up the rear."

Shepherd then broke in. "Alright people, we see the dome opening. How close are you?"

"We see it. Gillian, you're up." Ben called out.

Gillian's light fighter boosted up faster, and she made the run. First, she fired cannons, but no use. The bolts just bounced right off. The dome was halfway opened, and she could get a glimpse of the large barrel of the devastating cannon just inside. She targeted that barrel with her missiles, locked on, and fired.

To everyone's surprise, the rest of the dome shattered, and a giant explosion took place, and the giant cannon barrel blew out into space. The headset with shouts of joy.

Something happened then. Another dome began to open. "Kade, you're up next, just aim for the barrel," Gillian shouted.

Kade took his fighter in. He aimed for the barrel as it was coming out, and made a direct hit. There were no shouts of joy this time. There was yet another dome beginning to open. Saffron continued the attack and another hit.

"Scan for those domes underneath. How many more we got?" Ben said.

"I don't see another one opening."

"Admiral," came the voice of the Portman's Commander. "Their engines are boosting up, heading straight toward Cathia."

Shepherd watched out the viewport as the Bathshe ship started its run. "It's a suicide run. Take out that ship. Now."

Firing from all ships intensified toward the Bathshe ship. The shields were weakening, but it wasn't enough to take it out in time. The explosion on the planet could be seen from space. Luckily, after a probe re-con of the crash, it was determined that it had come down in an unpopulated area. But the damage zone still contained a small amount of radiation.

Nicolea watched Jon move slowly toward the buildings on his right side. The Bathshe hadn't noticed them yet. They seemed too busy building that strange structure. He was sweating, probably because of excited fear and heat. He heard Jon's voice in his earpiece.

"I'm here. Keep watch on them. Especially those big ones." It was said in a loud whisper.

"Keeping watch," Nicolea replied, hunkering down and looking through the scope on the rifle.

Jon crept out of the brush toward the grey structure. No windows but there was a door in the center. He removed his sidearm just before he slowly opened the door and peeked in. It was full of cots and portable lavatories lined up against the walls. Several clothing items were hung up in the two corners next to the door on the far wall.

In his loud whisper, he spoke in the mic to Nicolea. "Nothing here but a makeshift barracks. I'm going to make my way around to the larger building on the far side."

"Be careful, my friend. Those guys keep going in and out of it frequently. Don't get caught."

Jon thought for a moment, then removed one of the explosive devices out of his bag. "I have an idea. I'll plant two of the explosives on these two buildings as a decoy if something should happen. You're in charge of the boom."

Nicolea moaned slightly and pulled out one of the detonators from his own bag. He looked at the code. "It's set for 37-B."

Jon set the codes on two of the explosives and stuck them on the bottom of the buildings near the dirt ground. Then he moved back into the brush. "Okay, I'm moving. Explosives are set. Continue to keep watch."

"I'm watching." He was glad he was hidden. He liked Jon, even though they were from different factions. He respected him, but now he thought he was a bit crazy. "Don't get caught," he added.

Jon smiled and began the move slowly, not making any noise. He could hear the chatter from those working within the camp. Distinguishing between the men and the giants or Bathshe was easy. The voices of the Bathshe were almost scratchy, deep, and sounded like a mumble. It was almost scary sounding. It sent chills up his spine, but he had to get over it. He had a job to do.

Despite the increased likelihood of being seen, he was glad that he was the one doing the re-con. He couldn't imagine being Nicolea, sitting there in the brush, sweating and waiting for something to happen. Waiting for the boom. He trusted him with the detonator and with his life. They had just met, but there was something about him. Their personalities matched and perhaps in another world or time, they would have been partners, maybe friends. Maybe this was the beginning of a partnership.

Twenty minutes later, and he had made it to the larger grey building. So far, he was safe. "I made it," he reported back to Nicolea, who assured him the area still looked clear. There was a rear access here as well, but it resembled a utility access more than a door. Stooping low enough to accommodate his pack, he prepared to enter.

From what Nicolea saw through his scope, the giants had taken a seat on several of the nearby rocks and were engrossed in their own sort of conversation. He felt for the detonator with one hand just to make sure it was ready.

Jon made it through the opening as quietly as he could. There was some noise, but not enough to arouse suspicion. This building was different. This one had exotic building materials at one end. They had been picked through, probably being used to build that strange thing outside. He came across a table and on that table were what looked like plans of some kind. They didn't make much sense. He pulled out a personal ultralight scanner and used it to skim over the plans, barely finishing before he heard Nicolea's voice again.

"Two heading your way. Got a place to hide?"

Jon looked around, seeing nothing. A slight panic rippled through him. Then he said, taking a chance, "Blow it."

Nicolea took his eyes from the scope and reached and

grabbed the detonator and held it near the rifle butt. Then he heard Jon's voice again. "Blow it and see if you can take out some of those giants."

Without any hesitation, Nicolea did the job. He triggered the detonator, and the rear end of the two barracks jumped up in the sky in the explosive fires that were created. All eyes turned or looked up and watched it happen. The giants began running toward the buildings, ready for a fight. Nicolea aimed and took a shot at one of the giant's heads. Crimson smoke rose from the body and the head imploded. The smoke dissipated as the other giants turned toward their dead companion. Nicolea took quick shots again and again until all the giants had fallen.

In the chaos, he heard one of the men shouting. "Get the plans quickly!" The men ran into the bigger building, then he saw it explode, taking out half of the camp. The brush shield him somewhat from the heat, but he could feel the shockwave make the ground beneath him jump.

From around the rocks the giants had been sitting on came Jon, with his XL-9 rifle taking out the survivors before they could kill him. It was over in a moment.

"You can come on out, Nic, they're down."

Nicolea grabbed the gear and made his way into the clearing of the camp. He met Jon in the center, next to the device that was being built. "Find out what this is?"

Jon shook his head. "There were plans in that building. I just managed to make copies before I planted time-delay explosives on all four of the walls and get out. I say we just take photos of this thing and destroy it. We can't leave this thing laying around to be used for whatever it was actually going to be used for."

Nicolea grinned. "That's quite a mouthful."

Jon smiled back.

Three hours later they were on board the stealth ship, lifting off into the atmosphere. Jon jumped the ship into hyperspace and activated communications. "Who are you contacting?" Nicolea asked him.

"Synoa. Figured they need to know what we found."

"What if the communication is intercepted?"

Jon cracked a smile. "You forget. This is a stealth ship." Nicolea cocked his head in slight confusion, then smiled. He understood.

He proceeded with the communications to Synoa, and soon he was talking to Commander Dorman. After being apprised concerning their mission, Dorman spoke. "We need you to head to meet Shepherd en route. They need you ASAP. I'm sending you the coordinates."

"Something wrong?"

"You're heading to Deveron, to back up the Federation. All six of the Bathshe's second fleet are attacking."

Jon looked at Nicolea. "We're on our way."

Once they were aboard the Valiance, Jon sent the information he and Nicolea had gathered on Serenity to Synoa using an encrypted light code. After several moments of silence, the coded link from the President and Commander Dorman was on the screen.

Nicolea came in and sat next to him. The President was looking over the information that had been sent to him. Nicolea looked confused. "Where is Prime Minister Lamet?"

President Norris glared up. "The Prime Minister has a strong will. He's on the battlecruiser Vanquisher fighting over Deveron. The Federation commander requested that we send support."

Nicolea nodded and understood then. At least he would be able to fight for his Federation. He looked up again when President Norris cleared his throat and started to talk.

"I'm sending for Research and Development, maybe they can make something from these plans you copied. You guys have any ideas what this thing is?"

"Not a clue," Jon replied. "First thing that hit my mind was a doorway to something or somewhere else."

"Like a contained black hole kind of thing?"

Jon shrugged. "I don't know. It could be some kind of communications device as far as we know."

"Well, R and D will be here soon. I will let you know what it is as soon as we figure it out." There was a pause, and Dorman leaned and spoke something into his ear. "You guys get ready to fight. Defend Deveron with everything you have. It holds billions of people, innocent people. Save Deveron."

CHAPTER FOUR

The Electrik Connection

The planet below was unprotected. Planetary protections were not really necessary for this old world. Though it was still habitable, not much activity had taken place there for nearly 2000 years. Until today.

The Bird of Prey jumped back into normal space just above the planet and took its time to lower itself down to the edge of the atmosphere. Bjorn sat in the Captain's chair, waiting for the word that the orbit was locked in. He wondered what Gedor would do when he found out they had left. The way that arrogant admiral was doing things, he and the fleet would never reach their destination. Bjorn and his team had already arrived.

"The orbit is locked in." came the word from his pilot.

"Begin scanning for the target using the parameters Pan gave us."

"Yes, sir."

Bjorn smiled. It was about time things began to change in this known galaxy.

Around the same time, another ship jumped back into normal space around the world of Deveron and sent a message to the Federation battlecruiser Vanquisher.

"Vanquisher, this is the Republic battleship Valiance here to assist. What's the situation?"

"Valiance, we're glad to see you," came the reply. "We've destroyed half of the Bathshe fleet, but they are hitting us hard. And Prime Minister Lamet was in one of the corridors when it got hit. He's in the medical ward. We could use a shuttle to get him out of here." It was the voice of the Federation Commander Malcolm Astarte. "He shouldn't be here anyway."

Shepherd, then, got on the communications himself. "You got it. I'm sending your man with one of our own to pick him up in a long-range shuttle. We'll get him back to Synoa Station."

"Sounds like a plan," came Astarte's reply. Then they heard him give a quick order. "Get the Prime Minister to docking bay seven, and pull out of firing range. We need to get him out of here." Then back to Shepherd, he said, "We should be out of range in about five minutes. We'll have him ready."

Jon was standing behind Shepherd listening, as were the rest of the agents and Nicolea. "Jon said, "Come on, Nicolea, let's go."

Shepherd turned around. "Not you, Jon. I need you in a twin fighter with Ben. Saffron, you go with him, and get Prime Minister Lamet back to Synoa Station."

Saffron nodded, and Nicolea followed her out of the bridge. Admiral Shepherd spoke to the rest of the crew left on the bridge. To the Second Officer, he said, "Alert the crew to their battle stations." To the agents, he said, "get to your fighters. As soon as the shuttle departs, we're going full force into battle. We are going to save Deveron.

The long-range shuttle departed and headed for the damaged Federation Command ship as it came out of the battle zone. Saffron was in the back, preparing for the incoming. Nicolea was piloting, and as he came close, he made the comm call. "This is Dan in the rescue shuttle. Is the Prime Minister ready?"

"We're in the bay waiting, Dan," came the reply. "He is in a portable medical oxygen capsule."

Nicolea shouted back at Saffron. "Did you catch that Agent Baye?"

"Prepping now."

As they landed in the landing bay, the Valiance shot past the Vanquisher, ready for battle. Spewing from the battle bays on the dreadnought came the ship's complement of fighters. They too shot forward into action. Jon and Ben sat one behind the other in a twin Ikon fighter carrying heavy projectile missiles. After the fight at Cathia, Admiral Shepherd came prepared.

Jon was flying the twin fighter, and he was followed by the other agents. The Ikon singles were there to take out the Bathshe V-shaped fighters and keep them off their backs. "Okay Ben, keep your eyes peeled. Here we go." They then entered the battle zone.

Admiral Shepherd stood tall on the bridge looking out at the battle already waging ahead. One of the crewmen spoke up. "Admiral, we're getting a readout on Deveron. It's been hit hard, and is still being bombarded from the remaining Bathshe ships."

Shepherd pushed the comm button himself. "Agents,

take out those guns targeting the planet."

"We're on it," he heard Ben's voice reply.

Then he hit another button and connected to the shuttle. "How's the pickup coming?"

Nicolea came back on the speaker. "The Prime Minister is on board now, sir. We're about to leave."

"Good. Get Lamet back, and take him straight to the medical facilities there. They're the best."

The Valiance struck into battle, all guns blazing. This was going to be a rough one.

Thermonte Electrik, the Godfather of the Galaxy, sat in his large house, which overlooked a now mist-covered lake. It was morning on Chotis, and the fog covered mountains looked beautiful to him. He had always loved this location. He had lived here for years.

He sat in his entertainment room looking out the giant bay window at the lake and those mountains, and the small ship heading his way. In the den soft music played, and his mind wandered. He knew who was piloting the ship. It was Soshiana, the bio-tek, his only friend. Everyone else he was used to having around had left.

Several minutes later, Soshiana came into the room. With a drink in his hand, he took a casual sip. At least he could still enjoy the good life he was used to. "Did you find them?"

"I did." Soshiana walked further into the room and stood next to him. "I took the message personally. They knew who I was, and they didn't want me to leave. But I convinced them otherwise. They shall be here shortly."

Thermonte took another drink. He patted his own belly. "I'm getting fat," he said.

"You've been that way a while, sir," replied Soshiana. Thermonte just smiled. He started to think back on exactly what had started him down this path he was on.

It was dark outside, except for the blue lights flashing outside all around. He could hear movement downstairs in the deli and even up here in the apartment. In another room he could hear his mother crying.

Thermonte slid out of his bed onto his bare feet and walked over to the window. Locals were everywhere. He watched as a pair of paramedics carried out a body from his father's store, and then brought out others. He didn't know what was going on.

He quietly walked over to his bedroom door and opened it slightly. His mother was obviously on the other side of the apartment, by the crying he heard, but he did catch the voices of several of the inspectors.

"Where did you find him?" asked one of the men. Thermonte knew about Locals, and he knew this man was in charge. He had seen him before.

"In the back," replied the other man. "Looks like he was tortured. Arm in the grinder, and then shot twice, once in the thigh, and once in the head."

"Deli owner?"

"Yep. The wife said it was the Corlesh Clan. They had come back the other day to set up an appointment to use the deli, and Mr. Electrik agreed. When they came here for their appointment, they asked him to come down. And they killed him."

The man in charge thought for a moment. "You know it's going to be hard to get a conviction on this. The Corlesh have control of a lot of different things in the city. They own this city."

"What about her?" the inspector asked. "They may come back for her."

"We'll keep our eyes out. Best we can do. The Corlesh Clan won't hurt women and children. I will make sure of that."

After they had walked off, back down to the deli, Thermonte realized that they would do nothing. He hated the Corlesh Clan for killing his father, and he hated the Locals for not doing anything about it. Even at the age of eight, he would do whatever he had to do to get his revenge. He would get his revenge for his father with the Corlesh Clan. He would also get revenge for his *mother by dealing with the Locals.*

He opened his door and moved slowly toward his mother's room, where she was crying. The Locals had gone from the upstairs for the moment. Thermonte just crawled up next to her and hugged her. She held him back and continued to cry for the rest of the night.

He suddenly missed his father. He missed his mother as well, but they had spent more time together until she died. That was just before everything had changed.

Arnold Lamet, Prime Minister of the Federation, lay in the med bay. He had been through tests and surgery, but still lay unaware. He was alive, but his eyes had never opened. The medics called it a latent coma. Nicolea Dan stood just outside and looking through the glass. The room inside was sterile, and no one was allowed inside unless a medic went to check on him.

They had checked on him twice since he had been standing there. Saffron walked up behind him, placing a hand on his shoulder. "They are doing their best."

Silence came from Nicolea. He admired Lamet. He had been the best leader the Federation had ever had. And now his life was in the hands of Republic doctors.

"You know, our two sides may have different

government positions and maybe even different beliefs, philosophies, or ethics. But we both respect each other, and we keep the peace. And when true evil invades our space, we can come together to fight and help one another." Saffron continued, "These medics are the best. We will do anything to save him."

"I know," Nicolea replied. "It's just hard to see him this way. He has always been strong."

"He still is," assured Saffron. There was a short moment where they both just watched the Prime Minister. Then she remembered what she had come in to tell him. "The Valiance is back. You ready to find out what happened?" Nicolea nodded and turned to follow her back up to the base bridge.

The Valiant had little damage on the hull. Several of the cannon pods had been blown away, and one of the engines was offline. Battle scars peppered the shell, but there was no breach, and the shields were at fifteen percent. The dreadnought was much too big to dock with the station, so they sent a shuttle.

Admiral Shepherd and Jon Vega walked into the Synoa Station bridge where Commander Dorman waited for them. President Norris walked in soon after followed by Nicolea and Saffron. Then Commander

Astarte walked in behind them.

"So what is the verdict?" Norris asked.

Astarte moved ahead of them and answered the question. "It was brutal. Good news is, the entire fleet was taken out but we lost nearly all of our fleet. Deveron was sent back centuries and will take another century or two to rebuild. Seventy-five percent of it burned, and all the debris of the enemy fell to the surface. The capital city was destroyed."

"So, what now?"

"We still have a fight ahead of us," Dorman said. "We got to find out where they are going to hit next."

Jon agreed. "Then let's get patched up and get back out there."

President Norris looked over at General Brande, who had just walked in. Then looking back to Jon, he said, "Not you and Nicolea. You two have another mission."

Jon and Nicolea looked at one another. "You two follow me," the General said, "I'll tell you on the way."

They followed General Brande down the corridor. "I got a visitor from someone you know, Vega. You remember Mr. Electrik?"

"He left that house to come to see you? Did you arrest him?"

"He sent his associate, Soshiana," Brande replied. And he wants you to go and see him."

About what?" Jon asked. "How does he fit into all this?"

Nicolea looked confused. "Who is this, Mr. Electrik?"

"A gangster," answered Jon. "The biggest we have in the Republic."

"Apparently," Brande interrupted, "It has to do with what happened with Jonah."

"Jonah. That was six years ago."

"There has been an update since then."

"What is it?"

"Soshiana told me that he would only talk to you. I don't know. Only that it has to do with this war."

Jon had a bad feeling in his stomach. He should have known back then something was up. It was all just too neat. "When do we leave?"

"Right now. Take a long-range shuttle and meet the military transport Thrasher in the Satris System. When you are done talking to him, place him under house arrest, and Lieutenant Shane will watch him while you come back and report."

"He had better have answers," Jon said, and he and Nicolea headed on to the shuttle bay.

The Thrasher orbited the world of Chotis. Jon had been here before, six years previously. He had been here to talk to the same man about the terrorist and assassin known only as Jonah. Now Jon was here once again, to see the same man about the same terrorist and killer. He sat aboard the transport shuttle with a squad of marines and his new partner Nicolea Dan. Everyone was quiet as the shuttle lowered into the planet's atmosphere.

Nicolea was sitting next to him, and he broke the silence. "Is there anything I need to know about this Mr. Electrik? What is he like?"

"Very confident and very manipulative," Jon told him. "I would even say cocky. He knows we know he is a criminal, and he knows we have nothing on him and that all the things he is involved in cannot be proved."

"Nothing?"

Jon shook his head. "Not a shred."

"Sounds like we got something now though. Perhaps he's going to confess to us."

That made Jon chuckle. "Wait till you meet him. I doubt he will confess anything. He'll make it someone else's problem, and he just has news of it."

The shuttle soft-landed and Jon led the way followed by Nicolea and then the soldiers. Before they got to the door, Soshiana stepped out and closed the door behind her. Everyone stopped.

"What's all this?" she asked.

"Protection," Jon told her.

"They stay outside. He'll only talk to you."

"Why just me?"

"He trusts you," was her reply. She nodded to Nicolea. "Who's this? I don't know him."

Jon looked back at Nicolea, then back at her. "He is my new partner during this war. I trust him. He comes with me."

Soshiana looked him over carefully. "Okay, then. Just you two." She stepped back and opened the door.

Jon looked back at the soldiers. "We'll be back."

They followed Soshiana into the large house. Jon remembered this place, not much had changed. She led them down a couple of steps and into the den. Jon had also been in here before, with Saffron, when they took control of Jonah's remains.

They found Mr. Electrik sitting in his chair, which faced the giant windows overlooking the lake. "Jon Vega, my friend, thank you for coming." He noted

Nicolea. "Who's this?"

Nicolea stepped forward. "I am Nicolea Dan, Protector of the Federation."

"Well, well, this is different. The Republic and Federation working together." He laughed. "I guess there is something good coming out of this war after all." He gestured for them to sit down on the sofa, sitting opposite his chair. "Please have a seat."

Jon and Nicolea took a seat.

"You might hate me for this, but hear me out," Thermonte began, but Jon interrupted him.

"Jonah is alive."

Thermonte grimaced. "Yes and no."

"What do you mean?"

"Let me start from the beginning," Mr. Electrik said, "It will all make sense in the end."

"Go ahead."

"About ten years ago, I was contacted by a Doctor Phaleg. He had an opportunity for me, and that he would tell me about it once I arrived at his laboratory on a planet he called Dragmar."

"I've never heard of it," Jon said. He turned toward Nicolea, who indicated that he had no clue.

"I have the coordinates of this world," Thermonte

said. "The atmosphere of the world was harsh, but there is a laboratory. Anyway, back to my story. When I got there, Doctor Phaleg told me he wanted to send an expedition to a certain place where he said he had uncovered the border of water in space."

Jon looked confused. "Water in space?" So what is supposed to be on the other side of this border?"

To his surprise, it was Nicolea who spoke up. "It divides the firmament between this world and the next."

This didn't help Jon's confusion at all. "What world? Are you talking about this Dragmar?"

Thermonte smiled. He always seemed to smile when he could confuse someone. Especially an Agent. "Your friend gets it. He understands," he told Jon.

"Then make me understand," Jon told him.

Nicolea said, "It's a border between this reality and the celestial."

"You're talking about death, the afterlife."

Thermonte looked at Nicolea. "He might be beginning to understand."

Jon shook the thought out of his head. "Just finish this story, and what this has to do with Jonah."

"Very well. Inside the laboratory, Phaleg had this equipment that could physically change a person, right down to the color of the eyes and the fingerprints. He told me that he couldn't get the support of the Republic, nor could he get the funds to take on such an expedition. So he thought we could pool our resources together and use criminals with the promise of changing their physical selves. They would work for me on jobs, the first job being the expedition."

"To the water border in space," Jon said.

"That is correct."

Then Jon asked, "So, what body did I pick up that had his DNA on it?"

"That was my job," piped in Soshiana, who had been standing behind him the entire time. They had never even noticed.

"What do you mean?"

Thermonte Electrik smiled once again. "Don't tell me you didn't know, Jon. After all we've been through."

"What are you talking about?"

"Soshiana is my most loyal associate, my only friend. Look around Jon, " he gestured, "everyone left but her. Surely you did a scan on my house and surrounding property for life signs. It's your standard procedure."

"We did," Jon confirmed. "But what does it have to do with your best friend?"

The gangster looked up at his friend. Soshiana walked around the chair and stood in front of the sofa. "I am a bio-tek," she said quietly.

Jon looked at her, then at the smiling Electrik. Then he turned and looked at Nicolea. "Bio-teks have been illegal for over twenty-five years. They were considered unstable. They went mad."

"Doctor Phaleg fixed that problem. He gave me Soshiana to help me and to protect me if something went wrong."

Jon leaned back, rubbing his head. He finally had him on something illegal, but he couldn't do anything about it now. He had to think about the Bathshe, and arresting him now would put that in jeopardy. "Okay," he said, leaning forward, "what does the bio-tek have to do with Jonah's body?"

"Doctor Phaleg put extras in for me," Thermonte said. "You shake her hand, she can take a DNA sample. Doctor Phaleg also provided me with a cloning style machine, which could almost instantly create a human formed body from the DNA. No features or life, mind you, which is why we had to shoot him in the face."

"This Doctor Phaleg sounds like a good friend for you. Gave you everything you needed." Jon said. He was wondering if he needed to be angry. But he stayed on course. The war. "What does this have to do with the war?"

"Those men on those ships, most of them are ones I sent to Dragmar. Even Admiral Gedor. He was the first one I sent. I found him doing small assassination hits on Tiere of all places. He was an easy one. He took to it right away."

"And those ships?"

"I've never seen them before in my life," he told them. "It was three years after I sent Jonah to Dragmar when I found my associates dead all around the house. Soshiana cleaned up the mess."

"How do you know she didn't do it?" Nicolea asked him. Seemed an honest question.

"Because she is the one who killed the man who did. Never seen the man, or anything like him, before."

"What do you mean?"

"He was a giant. Only three fat fingers and a thumb, carrying an ax of some kind. He tore my men to shreds."

Jon and Nicolea looked at one another. They knew what they were, but said nothing. Thermonte continued.

"When these ships showed up and attacked Serenity,

and I heard Admiral Gedor's voice, I knew I had been betrayed. I tried to contact Doctor Phaleg on Dragmar and got no answer. I was angry because I was supposed to go on the exploration to the water border."

"Why didn't you go there yourself, and take a look around?" Jon asked.

"I figured I needed help. Protection, you might say. I obviously have no one here, except Soshiana. She is the only loyal person in my life, ever. My kids aren't even loyal to me. So that's why I contacted you. I didn't want to go there and die."

Jon looked at him. For the first time, he could see the sincerity in his face. He never even knew he had children. "This story seems fantastic, and I'm not even going to ask you how you could know it was Gedor. So tell me, what is it you really want?"

"I want to find out what really happened and how all this began. I don't want a war. That's bad for business."

Jon then said, "So that is the end of Jonah? You sent him off to this Dragmar?"

"After my men were killed, he contacted me, via vid-screen. The screen was blacked out, but I recognized his voice. He was still on the base on Dragmar.   He warned me not to report anything to anyone, or he would send more to kill me. So I stayed silent. Besides, I knew you wouldn't believe me. Look who I am and what people believe of me. They think I am a criminal."

"But you are."

Thermonte shrugged. "Maybe, maybe not. That has yet to be proved."

After a few moments, Nicolea leaned in and spoke to Jon. "We should go and report. Maybe they can make sense of all this."

Before Nicolea could stand, Jon, held him back. He had only one more question. "You said Jonah was going to be given a new look down to the eyes and the fingerprints. So did he have a new name?

"He had one, yes," Thermonte said to him. "He goes by the name of Andrelus Pan. And he seems to be in charge now."

They stood up, realizing Soshiana was guiding them to the door. To Mr. Electrik, Jon said, "We are going to leave the soldiers here, for your protection, and to make sure you don't leave without us knowing. And how about giving us the coordinates to this Dragmar?"

"You will get them as soon as you come back. We'll take my yacht when we go."

Jon sighed. There was no point in arguing with him,

but maybe command would be able to come up with something. After making sure the lieutenant had all the supplies and men he would need Jon and Nicolea left. When their shuttle rejoined the Thrasher they all headed back to Synoa Station.

Once on board, Nicolea noticed Jon was very quiet. "You alright man?"

"I hate that man. I wanted to kill him."

"Then you would have been no better than this Jonah character."

Jon looked at him. He wasn't smiling. "I know. We need him. That is the only reason I didn't kill him." They looked at one another in silence for a moment. Then he continued. "He tricked me once, but not again. If Thermonte Electrik even thinks about betraying me again, making a fool of us, I won't hesitate."

"If he betrays us," Nicolea said, "I'll step aside for you."

Jon nodded and looked ahead as they walked back to the bridge of the ship.

CHAPTER FIVE
Shepherd Of The Stars

The comm buzzed, waking Shepherd out of deep sleep. It had to be at least the second or third buzz. At first, he had sleepily thought it was an alarm. He sat up quickly after he realized what it was and answered. "This is Shepherd."

"Sir, sensors show five Bathshe ships just entering the Bel Terra System," came the reply.

He ran his hand through his short white hair. "I'm on my way."

After getting dressed, he walked out into the corridor and made his way up to the bridge, where he was met by his second officer. "Sir, the officer asked, "how did you know they would show up at Bel Terra?"

"If they were going to hit Tiere, they would have done it already. Too much time had passed." He looked at the radar monitoring the enemy fleet. "Did you send the signal?"

"As soon as we saw them, sir."

"How much time?"

"Twelve hours give or take. They are moving in slow."

"It's Admiral Gedor," Shepherd said. "He's confident. How long before the others get here?"

"Four hours, if they leave right away."

Shepherd thought for a moment. He knew what was going on and he knew why they were here over Bel Terra. His greatest fear was this moment. "First order of business when the fleet gets here is to create a barrier between them and the planet. Get the fighters we have ready to launch."

"Sir, we have a ship that just jumped in close by."

Then the comm buzzed, and the incoming voices from the new ship he recognized. "This is stealth ship SC-4, request permission to dock. Sending codes now."

"SC-4, your codes have been verified." the officer reported back to them. "Docking orders are being relayed as we speak."

Shepherd turned back before walking out the door.

"Tell them to meet me in the rec room, alone."

"Yes, sir."

With that, he left the bridge and headed to meet Jon and Nicolea. His mind flipped through his past. A past long before this present existed. No one here knew about it, nor would any man here know about it. This was his second chance to do more good for this world, and he knew there would not be another. It was what Lenok told him back after he saved him on the sky city of Rathion.

It was when he was leaving for this world. He said, "You will not be able to return here. This will be your last term of life."

Shepherd knew it was time. He made sure the rec room was empty, then took a chair at one of the tables in the middle of the room. He took a moment to pray. Then Jon and Nicolea walked into the room, and he offered them a chair at the table.

"What's up, Admiral?" Jon asked as they both sat down.

Grand Admiral Shepherd sighed. Then he began. "I need you two to be ready for a mission. And I want your promise, your guarantee, that you will obey me when I give you the order to begin the mission."

"What's the mission?" Jon asked him. Shepherd widened his eyes and continued that stern look at him. "Okay," he said, then he looked at Nicolea, who nodded. "We agree."

Admiral Shepherd leaned back in the chair and started. "We are about to have a big fight, as you can tell. Sometime during that fight, if things start to go bad, I want you and Nicolea to take the stealth ship and head to Bel Terra, specifically the northern shores of the continent of Connish. There you will be met by a man who will take you to another man. From then on out, you will do as the second man says. Am I understood?"

"Sir," Jon protested, "if things start to go bad, won't you will need us here?"

Sternly, Shepherd replied, "if things start to go bad, you will do exactly as I say. Is that understood?"

Jon looked over at Nicolea, with whom he had become good friends during this ordeal. They trusted one another. Without saying a word, they seemed to agree on the one thing they needed to decide on. Jon looked back at his superior. "Understood. We are not going to like it, but we will do this mission."

Shepherd stood up and started to head out of the room. Jon and Nicolea stood also. "Sir," Jon said, "I hope you know what you are doing."

The admiral glanced back. A moment passed. "Come on. The others are here. They arrived early. Perhaps this will be a good day after all."

He walked out, and they followed. When they reached the bridge, they found it was not the others Shepherd had sent for, but it was seven battleships from the Federation. The admiral allowed a slight grin to fall across his face. A call came in from the ship.

"Well, Grand Admiral Shepherd, this is Commander Astarte of the battleship Vanquisher, of the Federation Navy. We are here to help."

Nicolea had a broad smile across his face. He was glad and proud that Astarte was here. He had that smile all through the conversation between the two fleet commanders.

"Commander Astarte, we are honored you are here to help. I figured you would be helping with the damage on Deveron."

"We have other ships for that task. We feel we have to end this together so we can heal together. Both of our governments."

There was a moment of silence, but mostly of relief. "Well then," Shepherd said, "let's get started."

"What's first, Grand Admiral?" asked Astarte.

"First, we need to create a blockade to force a battle. The rest of our fleet should be here soon."

"You are in charge," Astarte stated. "Let's end this."

Admiral Gedor stood on the bridge of his command ship watching the stars move past them. He had just gotten the word about the other vessels ahead. They had formed a blockade in front of Bel Terra, and he had five of the best battleships on his side. Those rundown dregs ahead would crumble before him. The master's plan would be fulfilled.

"Speed up," he commanded. "Let's get this over with. It's time to conquer."

The five Bathshe battleships doubled their speed. Shepherd saw the enemy fleet do so. He reached in his top pocket and pulled out a small leather journal wrapped in thin twine. This had to be saved. This information was about the age where cities floated in the sky, during the war. When he was someone else, before he was known as Shepherd.

He called over a guard from the doorway leading onto the bridge. "Take this to Agent Vega down in the bay." He handed it over to the guard. "Tell him to give it to the man he is supposed to meet. If Vega refuses, tell him that if we get through this, he can give it back. I just need it safe."

"Yes, sir," the guard nodded, before turning to leave.

Shepherd got back to what lay ahead. The fight that would make or break this version of the world he was in now. He hoped Lenok would be able to use it for the future. He also hoped that his own fleet would make it in time. Then he had an idea, but it depended on how far along Commander Stone and the rest of the fleet were.

"Get me the battlecruiser Defender. I want to speak to Commander Stone on a secure line, double coded."

"Yes, sir," reported the officer.

The seven Federation battleships were now in place waiting for the Bathshe. They were probably here for revenge for nearly destroying their own capital world. He really didn't blame them for it, although he knew it was the wrong reason. But at the moment, he would take what he could get. At least they knew that he would be in charge. The one thing this invasion had done was to bring the two factions together. Maybe this would all be good for them in the long run.

"Sir, I have Commander Stone on comms. I actually triple coded it, sir." Shepherd stared at him for a moment before he gave him a slight smile. They all knew how important this fight was. The officer smiled back. "No point in taking chances."

Shepherd nodded to receive. "Commander Stone," he said after the comms were lit. "This is Admiral Shepherd. How far away are you from us?"

There was a brief silence. "We are about three more hours out, sir."

That was almost good enough. "I need you to do something for me, Commander."

Bjorn Chelli watched as one of his men walked up to him. He was filthy with the soil around him. Bjorn could smell him as he walked out of the thick brush which grew up around the forest around them. A forest so dense, it nearly removed the light shining down from the sun.

"We think we found it," the man said.

"You think. We need to be sure."

"Well, we found an opening, still mostly covered with those large roots. We dropped in a rock in, heard nothing. Lights show nothing but more darkness."

Bjorn nodded in agreement. This was it. "Get the saw blades going, and remove those roots. Leave that tree where the hole is, and remove those around it. They will be here soon."

Shepherd looked out of the viewport on the bridge. The Bathshe fleet was closer, he could see them now. They were moving in faster, a little bit too soon. "Are they in range for a scan yet?"

"Not yet, sir." replied the officer. "They'll be here in about fifteen minutes."

"Alert the fighters and contact Astarte. We need to be ready."

Down in the stealth ship, Jon and Nicolea heard the alert for the fighters to prepare to launch. This was it. Jon was ready. It was time to get into the fight. Then he heard to comms buzz.

Jon answered it. It was Shepherd. "We're ready sir."

"I need you to head on to the coordinates now," replied the admiral.

"Admiral, you will need us in the fight," Jon protested. "We're not leaving."

Shepherd got stern. "This is an order, Agent. Or I

will turn you in for insubordination."

"Sir..."

"Jon," the admiral began. "Go. I have this covered. They won't know what hit them."

"But sir?"

"Just go, Jon. Trust me. Your mission is more important than this fight. It could actually change the outcome."

Jon took a moment to think about it. "We'll go. But you keep yourself safe, Admiral."

"Don't worry about us here." Shepherd looked out the viewport again. "Make sure you give that journal to that man I told you about. It's important."

"Yes sir," Jon replied, then started up the engines of the stealth ship and left the bay into space and down to Bel Terra.

The stealth ship left the bay, and the admiral watched it head down to the world below. He had been there at one time, and he remembered when he had first met Lenok. He had even read what had been written in the scrolls.

It had been twelve years since Habor Pan had fallen and the Nation of Machonon was divided, and for the time, all seemed peaceful. Marat left the city with the food for the shopping list

Heather had given him. At home, his son, now seventeen, watched on the veranda of the house for his father.

The house came into view and Nathan waved. It made Marat smile. Finally, he thought, it seemed he had a normal life, or as normal as it could be in the times. As he came closer, Nathan ran out to help him, grabbing the groceries from his father's hands. "Mom's been waiting on you; she already has started dinner."

"So what are we having this evening, one of your mom's special surprises?"

They both laughed. Nathan had always looked up to his father, not only for the deeds he had done but also for the way he honored his mother. Even in joking, he knew his father loved his mother. He wanted to be like him. "I think I started dating Sara today," he told him.

"You think you are dating?"

"We talked about it." Nathan paused for a moment. "We did start dating, dad."

"Sara is a nice girl and comes from a good family. Treat her well, and if you become closer, then give her your respect and put her first in your life, after God."

They reached the house, and suddenly Marat felt an intense heat burning within him. He dropped the basket of fruit in his hands and fell to his knees. He grasped his heart. Nathan ran to get his mom, and Marat felt a hand on his shoulder.

"It's time, Marat. I have come to take you home."

Marat looked up and saw the White Seraph waiting. "The piece of me I gave you is about to burn you up. It is time to take it back."

"I need time to say goodbye," he said. "Can I have a few more moments?"

The White Seraph placed his hand over Marat's heart to calm the burning. "I will be waiting in the place where we first met. Don't take too long." Then he was gone.

Heather followed her son out onto the veranda, where Marat was just getting back up. "Nathan said you fell to the ground, what happened?"

Marat looked into his wife's eyes for what seemed to be an eternity. "It's time for me to go, my love. I am being called home."

"What do you mean called home?" Nathan asked. "You are home."

He placed a hand on his son's shoulder. "I am being called home to the Lord."

Tears began to swell up in both Heather and Nathan's eyes. She knew what he meant, for she was there when the White Seraph had appeared so many years ago. Nathan knew nothing, but she would tell him later in the future. She fell into his arms, *hugging him she knew for the last time.*

Marat pulled his son in close. "This needs to happen, Nathan. Do not fear this, nor do not weep for me, son. I want you to take care of your mother, be strong, and continue to follow the Lord."

"I love you, dad."

"I love you too, son."

Nathan gave his father one last hug and stepped away. Marat looked down at Heather and wiped the tears from her face. "I will always love you and will be waiting for you. You teach our son well. Everything will be fine."

"I love you so very much, too." She pulled his head down, and she gave him a long loving kiss.

After several moments, they pulled away. Heather pulled Nathan in close, and they both watched their husband and father walk down the path. Soon he disappeared over the horizon, and they never saw him again.

Before Nathan and his mom walked back into the house, they saw a figure appear, wearing a brown robe, heading toward them. He was an older man, bearded in a grey beard; they watched as he came closer. "Are you Nathan, son of Marat?"

Nathan looked up at his mother. Her face revealed nothing of this. She knew not what was going on. Finally, he replied, "Yes, I am Nathan."

The old man smiled. "I have a message for you. A message from the God of Light."

He wondered then if he would see his father on the other side. He was interrupted by the officer monitoring the sensors.

"Sir, They are almost in range."

"Prepare to launch fighters."

Admiral Gedor stood proudly on the bridge of his ship. Nothing was going to stop them. He would be the greatest tactician in the galaxy. It was time to defeat Shepherd once and for all. Time to take control of the universe, and to create his empire.

"Admiral," spoke the sensor officer, "we have multiple incoming."

"Where?"

"They're coming in below us, sir."

Gedor felt a wave of anxiety than anger flow through him. "NO!!" he shouted. He should have known Shepherd would pull a stunt like this. "Launch all fighters, and point all heavy cannons toward the incoming ships now."

At that moment the Republic fleet jumped in, cannons firing on the underbelly of the Bathshe fleet. Many of the Bathshe fighters had escaped the bays of two of the exploding ships located on the back end of the enemy battle fleet. Then the heavy cannons began firing onto Commander Stone's fleet, and he ordered the launching of fighters.

The lead on these fighters was Saffron Baye, and she had her orders. It was the same as before, moving in to destroy those cannons.

Commander Astarte and the Federation fleet moved forward to attack the front of the Bathshe. All fighters were being launched, and it became a chaotic battlefield. Shepherd watched all this, and he hated seeing this. He had seen it before and had not taken the steps necessary to stop it. But this time, Shepherd knew he had no choice. He had to give Jon and Nicolea a chance to fix it. No one knew it, but it was all in their hands now.

"Get me Commander Astarte, now," he ordered, and soon the Commander was on with him.

"Yes, Admiral?"

"Pull your ship back next to the Valiance. I'm sending you my crew, then get your fleet out of here."

"Run from a fight, Admiral?"

"Finishing the fight, Commander."

There was a pause. There was respect between the two fleet commanders now. Then Astarte replied. "May the Lord of Light be with you, Shepherd."

When the call ended, the entire bridge crew was looking at him. He looked around, taking his time to meet all their eyes. He said, "My orders will be obeyed. Prepare the crew for the transfer, and then go yourselves. Lieutenant Baker, I need you to find the ship Gedor is on."

Baker rushed over the computer and began the search. Shepherd looked around the bridge. "Let's get moving people. Now." Everyone started their work and slowly began leaving the room one by one.

"Admiral, I found one ship that has a triple shield generating around it. The others just have a single."

That was him. He knew Gedor was a coward and would do anything to ensure that he survived. He handed Baker a small folder he had pulled out of his jacket pocket. "Give this to Commander Astarte. It is his orders on what to do next."

"Get me a comm open to Commander Stone, then get off this ship, Lieutenant." Baker did as he was told, then left Shepherd alone on the bridge.

Three of the five Bathshe battleships had been taken out, two of them having been destroyed entirely by Stone's fleet. Two of his fleet had also been severely damaged, and those crews were being taken on board another ship. Saffron flew her fighter weaving in and out of the battle, taking out the closest Bathshe fighters that came near her. She was one of the best.

Her comms buzzed. It was Stone. "Hey Saff, go ahead, and you and your team do as much damage as you can to the ship on these coordinates, and then get back here quick."

"What about that last ship, sir?"

"Its orders, agent," Stone replied. "I'm pulling the others back now."

On board the Bathshe flagship, Gedor's eyes were wide in anticipation watching the battle unfold out of his viewport. Then he noticed it. "Look, they're pulling away. We're winning. Bel Terra is ours!" Inside he was humming. He had beaten Shepherd, even after that trick he had pulled. But the smile didn't last long.

It was the Valiance, Shepherd's command ship. It was moving forward, every gun he had blazing toward them. The bolts were just being absorbed by the energy shields around them. Gedor relaxed. "Aim everything we got toward the Valiance" he ordered. "Take out that ship."

Grand Admiral Shepherd sat at the pilot seat on the bridge. He had already targeted the Bathshe flagship with every gun he had and begun to fire even before he had started moving. He was slowly moving closer and closer, then the ship started to shoot back. The energy shots from the Bathshe ship were not yet penetrating the Valiance's shields, but as he moved toward the Bathshe, the shields would begin to fail, and damage would accumulate. He knew that the Bathshe ship had three separate shields. His cannons would not be able to destroy the Bathshe ship in time. He also knew that Gedor would not be satisfied in just taking over Bel Terra, but would utterly destroy it. That would not happen.

He looked out the viewport and watched Commander Stone's fleet moving away. The Federation fleet was already gone, jumping quickly to perform their last order. With everything now in place, he increased his speed. First, it was slow as he was saying his final prayer to the Lord or the Light, the one true God of the galaxy and of mankind. As he closed his prayer, and the Valiance was already taking hits, he increased the speed to full throttle.

Admiral Gedor only had time to widen his eyes before

he knew what was happening. The Valiance penetrated the three shields easily and crashed into the Bathshe ship, causing a massive explosion that could be seen from Bel Terra's surface.

Jon and Nicolea had just stepped off their ship when they heard, then saw, the explosion nearly above them. They both looked up and just watched.

The second Bathshe ship that Saffron successfully knocked out got caught in the explosion and a piece of the flagship shot out and caused another explosion when it collided with it. The only thing left was floating debris.

Commander Stone watched from a distance. The invasion was over, and so much had been lost. So many deaths. There was one thing good that had come out of it. It had brought two conflicting sides together as friends, and maybe the Lord willing, they would stay friends. There was always a reason things happened or were allowed to happen.

He thought about Shepherd's last command to him. He knew Shepherd had always had insight into strategies, which is why he was such a great commander. He also knew that he was a believer. He had peace that Admiral Shepherd had known what he was doing was best.

With that thought, he gave the order to jump into light speed and head back to Synoa Station.

CHAPTER SIX
The Prophet Warrior

It was a cold night. The sun had set several hours earlier, and it was the small campfire that illuminated their faces and kept them warm. The explosion they had seen in the sky Jon knew was a collision. He had seen one before. There was always that first big explosion, followed by smaller explosions and debris falling through the atmosphere. Shepherd had sacrificed himself. He had respected Shepherd, and he felt sick when he had understood.

"You might want to get you some sleep, Jon," Nicolea said. There was no answer from his colleague. "You know he did what he did to save us all."

"There had to be something I could have done to

help. Maybe we could have saved him."

"There are things in this universe that cannot be helped, and things that have to be done for the good of others. Do you believe that?"

Jon thought for a moment. He didn't know how to answer that. Jon was a man of action, and he felt he had taken the coward's way out. He had run from a fight. The fight that took Admiral Shepherd's life. "What good could have come about with Shepherd's death?"

"Perhaps we will find out," Nicolea told him. "I know where we are going. I have read about it in the Book of Light. It's a holy place to some, but it's mainly a place that is between this world and the celestial world."

This made Jon chuckle a bit. He had heard the children's stories from that book when he was young. His parents had taken him to church then but he had never thought of going once he joined the military. From there he had become an Agent of the Republic. A duty he had taken very seriously. "Are you making this about religion?"

"Jon, have you ever thought about where we come from and where we go after we pass from this world?"

"Look, Nicolea, I have the utmost respect for you and your beliefs, but I don't really feel like hearing this right now."

Nicolea backed off. He nodded and took another drink of the water from his bottle. There was food storage on the ship they had landed in. "Okay, Jon. Maybe we'll talk later about it when you're feeling up to it."

Jon stayed quiet, but he nodded an agreement. He stood up and started heading back to the ship. "I'm going to get some sleep. See you in the morning."

Nicolea watched him leave and stayed by the fire until it was burning in ashes.

The following morning when Nicolea walked out of the ship there stood a man near the shore dressed in a light brown cloak. The only hair visible under his hood was a neatly trimmed white beard. The man was silent, just watching and waiting.

Nicolea called back up to Jon, who came down and saw the man. "Who is he?"

Nicolea shrugged. "Let's go find out."

Before they moved toward the man, Jon made it a point to grab a small pistol he had kept just inside the hatchway before securing the ship. They walked side by side, unsure of what to expect from the stranger that was still there watching them.

"Can we help you?" Jon asked. His voice was calm, but Nicolea saw that his hand stayed close to the pistol.

The man smiled slightly knowing that these two men were suspicious. "I am called Rosha," he said. "I am to take you to the island."

"What island?"

"You were invited to the Isle of Illosha, were you not?"

Jon and Nicolea looked at one another. Invited? They both seemed to be thinking about it. It was Jon who replied back to him. "We were sent here by our commanding officer to meet a man."

"Specifically to meet a man who will take us to another man," Nicolea added.

Rosha smiled wider then. "Yes, I know. Come on, the boat is here. I am the first man, and I will take you to the other man."

The boatman turned toward the small boat sitting on the shore. It looked like a small gondola with a large oar leaned against the white boat. He paused when he saw the two men still standing. "Well hurry up. The Prophet Warrior will not wait forever."

Nicolea started to move ahead first, followed closely by Jon. "What's a Prophet Warrior?" he asked Nicolea.

"I assume we are about to find out," was his reply. He had only heard of them in the ancient time from his time in the Temple of Light back on the world of Deveron when he was growing up. He hadn't really thought they existed today.

They climbed in the boat and sat one in front of the other looking out over the sea. Rosha stood on the small platform in the back, took hold of the oar, and pushed away from the shore. Slowly but steadily they moved out into the open sea, small waves trying to push them back, but to no avail. After about fifteen minutes, a strange mist began to close in around them, hiding them from the shore.

From the shore, on the far side of the sands, a man watched through long-range binoculars as the boat vanished. He looked back at the stealth ship for a moment. Then he grabbed his radio and spoke into it.

"Tell Bjorn that the men are here. They have left out into the sea, but their ship is still here. I will await orders."

"This is Bjorn," came the reply. "Everything here is ready, and we're heading out now to meet at your location. Let me know if anything changes."

"Yes, sir. Jenson out."

When the mist cleared, they found themselves in a small cove of the island. Jon and Nicolea were both in awe; words left them at the beauty of the island. Ahead of them there was a small beach of white sands surrounded by what seemed a garden, a paradise. An oasis of vegetation with large, perfectly constructed trees and well-trimmed bushes. They felt a light breeze, not too cold, but almost warm. The boat continued to move steadily toward the white beaches.

"Is this what I believe it is?" Nicolea asked.

"This is Illosha," the boatman answered. "The Isle of Paradise, where it all began."

Jon turned to his partner. "Where what began?"

"Us." It was Nicolea's only answer.

As they came closer, they saw a man emerge from the trees behind the sands and walk closer to the beach. He was dressed in robes, much like the boatman's, only the man's robes were lighter. He walked with a staff, and his hair was shoulder length and grey, as was his well-trimmed beard. Supple leather sandals covered his feet.

"Who is that?" Jon asked Rosha.

Rosha smiled. "That my friends is the other man whom you are to see."

The boat glided softly onto the sands, and the two men stepped out. "Welcome to Illosha, Jon Vega and Nicolea Dan. It is always nice to have visitors here in paradise. My name is Lenok."

"You know our names?" This almost made Jon uncomfortable.

"Of course, I know a lot about you." He looked at Nicolea and smiled, giving him a quick nod. "I am particularly happy to finally meet you, sir. We have a lot to talk about."

Then Jon remembered the book Shepherd had given him. He took it out. "I was told to give this to you."

Lenok took it and looked at it. "The Shepherd remembered."

Jon was taken back. "The Shepherd? His name was Shepherd. He was our Grand Admiral of our entire military force."

Lenok nodded up and down. "Yes, that is who he was when you knew him. His name was Nathan, son of Marat. He had been chosen to be a Shepherd when he was young and took it as his surname. He was a man of honor."

"And the journal?" Jon was curious now. "What's in that?"

"History, my friend. History of his life and the world around him." They all stood for a moment in silence. "Come on, let us head into the village. And you can tell me why you are here."

They began to walk away from the sea and onto a neatly made trail. It was leading into the forest ahead of them. Lenok began to talk. "Shall I give you a little bit of history of the island? We have time before we reach the village."

"I would love to hear it." Nicolea put in before Jon could say anything. He had heard of it before in his teaching in the temple. As a youth he had often wished he had lived through those times. Even now, he felt at home here on the island.

"This is the garden where God created the first man and the first woman from the dust of the ground. Their eyes were uncovered then, and they could see and speak with God here, as the Lord walked among them. Then the seraph Pan, who had grown jealous of mankind, came into the garden and tempted them, and sin entered into their lives. They were cast out into the mainland,

and their eyes were closed, and they could no longer see God or understand his words.

"God closed the pathway that linked the celestial and the physical, and in time, he used the seraphs to help mankind. But the seraph Pan had corrupted other seraphs, and God sent them away from His throne. They had become the fallen seraphs, and hence a division began. Those who followed Pan became known as the Dark Seraphs, and those who remained obedient to God were known as the White Seraphs."

Lenok paused for a moment. They passed two giant oaks standing several feet apart alone in a circular clearing. Between the two trees was a dark liquid substance that rose up the length of the trees to the very tops.

"What is that?" Jon asked, pointing, and the others stopped and looked.

"That is the barrier God constructed between the celestial and the physical," Lenok told him, and Jon moved closer toward it. "Go ahead, touch it. It will not hurt you."

Jon touched it, and a small ripple came from the touch. "It's water," he stated.

"Yes."

"Why is it so dark?" he asked.

"Because it is deep, very deep. If you tried to pass through it, your flesh would perish."

As he walked away from the water, Jon looked intently at Lenok. "The boatman told us you are a Prophet Warrior. What is that?"

"I was brought here from a young age to prophesy to mankind throughout the times and to fight like a seraph if need be. A man cannot defeat me."

"Is that why you wear those robes, like a uniform?"

Lenok smiled again. This one had much to learn and to understand. But there was a reason he was brought here. He said, "There are many others, all wearing the clothing of the era they came from. The man you knew as Shepherd, for instance, wore a uniform as you say. But not from this era."

They started walking down the path again, and Jon asked another question. "So just how long have you been here?"

"Do you recollect the tale of the evil king, Kief Dan?"

The name hit a nerve with Nicolea. Same surname, same ancestry. He knew the name from Temple class when he was younger. "Was he my ancestor?" he blurted out. He had stopped to wait for an answer.

Without stopping, Lenok said, "Yes, he was." He turned his head around and motioned with his staff at him. "Come on, and you will learn the truth of the peoples of Dan."

Nicolea slowly started to move ahead. Lenok continued. "Now Jon, have you ever heard of this King Kief Dan?"

Jon vaguely remembered something about it. "He was murdered by his wife long ago, in ancient times, so I understand. Why are you asking me this?"

"That was my first purpose as a Prophet Warrior."

"But you only look to be in your forties, maybe fifty."

The Prophet Warrior laughed out loud then. "Why thank you, sir, it's almost comforting to hear you say that. But in reality, time has no meaning here. We age slowly, yes, when on a mission, but everyone here is much older than you would think. Except for you two. It's been a long time since we had guests."

Soon they entered an open area surrounded by huts around the edge. The huts seemed almost as if the forest had grown them where they stood. A large wooden table, surrounded by wooden chairs, stood in the center of the clearing. Lenok pointed to one of the huts. "That will be for you to rest or sleep if you like.

And when you are ready, you can tell me why you are here."

"We're ready now," Jon said.

"First, I need to go to the library, and get some texts for you." He was looking at Nicolea. "It will help you understand your ancestry." Then to Jon, he said, "We have time." Then he left down another path and disappeared into the brush and trees.

It took twelve hours for Bjorn to make his way to the Northern Shores where the stealth ship sat on the beach. Jenson greeted him with a handshake, and then he looked through the field glasses he carried with him. He was looking at the exact spot where Jenson said the boatman had appeared.

"When do you think they'll be back?" Bjorn asked.

"Who knows?"

On the beach, fifteen men, and a few giants, started to set up camp on the beach. Bjorn turned to his friend. "We'll just have to wait for them to come back. Set up a scope here, and keep a man up here all the time. I need a warning when the boat shows back up."

"You got it."

Jon could not sleep. One reason was that the sun never seemed to set on this island, and it was still light outside his hut. However, the main reason was that his mind was still working and working hard. Grasping this place was hard. He stood up and walked out of the hut.

Jon saw Lenok sitting alone at the massive table. Jon walked up to him and sat down across the table. "So where is Nicolea?"

"I gave him a couple of scrolls he needs to read," replied Lenok. "He had questions about his heritage. I hope they help."

"So why are we still here? I was sent to give you a journal from Admiral Shepherd, and that was it. He said you could help us with a problem."

"Tell me about your problem."

"I assume you know all, like about Mr. Electrik?"

Lenok smiled. "We don't know all, which is why we have people like your Admiral Shepherd out there, to help us preserve the true history of this world. But to answer your question, we do know of Thermonte Electrik. His entire life, in fact."

"I don't trust him," Jon replied.

"The God of Light will use all to achieve his purpose, even if they don't believe. So Thermonte Electrik still has a purpose, whether he is lying or not." He watched as Jon was thinking about this. Then he said, "What about you, Jon Vega? Do you believe in the Light?"

"I believe that some men are good, and some men are evil. I have come to understand that evil is a man.

CHAPTER SEVEN
First Scroll of Dan

The stag stopped slowly in front of them, looked around, and bent down to eat. Lesh looked up from the giant fallen tree at the animal and then to his friend, lying there beside him. "There is a fine animal. It would make a great offering."

Kief Dan then looked up. "This one is mine," he said, "I haven't had a kill all day, and you have several rabbits in your bag."

Lesh smiled. "All right, he is all yours, brother Kief. However, you had better not miss, or I will be taking the shot.

Kief Dan rose up on his knees from behind the log and drew back his bow. 'I will not miss." As the arrow was slowly pulled back, the sound was picked up by the stag's ear, and its head lifted, and its ears perked.

As the arrow was released from the bow, the stag took off, and he missed. Lesh quickly stood up and drew back his bow, firing an arrow at the animal as it ran. The bolt hit the base of the stag's neck, and down it fell.

"Sorry brother," he told Kief Dan. "I got this one."

Kief grumbled as he followed Lesh to the fallen animal. Then he heard a rustling in the brush next to him, and another stag walked out. Pulling out his bow, Kief quickly took another arrow and drew his bow and fired. The bolt hit the stag just below the front of his neck, and it fell dead.

Lesh watched in amazement as the whole scene took place. "Nice shot, brother Kief. That one is bigger than mine. That is going to be a fine offering to the Lord."

"It will also make a good feast for the oncoming winter."

Lesh stood up and patted him on the shoulder. "Tell you what, I will share my rabbits with you so that you will have food, but the Lord deserves the best."

Kief looked at him. "I suppose you're right." He accepted the two rabbits from his friend and put them in his sack. Then they picked up their individual kills and headed back to their home. As they were leaving, a shadowed figure stepped out from the forest and watched the two leave. As the wind picked up the shadow stretched out and vanished.

The people of Gal-Gilead were proud people, living off the land. They enjoyed a good life, and were a peaceful people, never going to war against the other peoples of Connacht. Connacht was ruled by King Alic from New Galmesh, which was the largest city in the land. In the village of Janish, in the central part of Gal-Gilead, Kief Dan and Lesh carried in their kills from the forest near the Mountain Road. It was nothing new to see them coming home with kills, and they were not the only ones doing so. All throughout the day, men of Janish were bringing in their kills and their offerings for the Lord. These two were only more hunters walking doing the same.

"I suppose we should go home and prepare our offerings and dinner," Lesh said to his friend.

Kief Dan laughed. "You have a wife to cook your dinner, and prepare your offering."

Smiling, Lesh said, "My wife makes the dinner, but I do prepare the offering, as it should be. Besides, you'll find a wife soon enough. Gal-Gilead is filled with women wanting to marry."

"Not as good as Sareen, I suspect."

"Brother Kief, remember it's what is on the inside that counts, not the outside."

Kief nodded in agreement, but his thoughts were otherwise. Lesh's wife Sareen was one of the most beautiful women in Gal-

Gilead, and probably Connacht. He sometimes wished he had gotten to her first. "Well, I had better get home," he told Lesh. "I will see you tomorrow."

Both went their separate ways. Kief watched as Lesh met Sareen just a few feet away and kissed her. She took his bag to lighten his load, and they walked together to their home. Kief turned and went into his own house, throwing the stag on the long table just inside. Then he heard someone behind him. He began to see a shadowed figure standing there like wind blowing. Kief was startled. "Who are you?" he asked.

The figure stood there in silence for a moment. Then the words came in a whispery voice. "I am known by many names in many different cultures, many different lands. However, you can call me Dagon."

"What do you want?"

"Why do you put up with Lesh?"

"He is my friend."

"He has everything you want, everything that should be yours. Has this Lord you follow given you what you want?" the shadowed figure asked. "Everything you want has been taken from you, and given to Lesh. Even the kills from your hunt today."

Kief looked at the stag on the table. "I killed the stag. It's my kill."

"And yet you have to give it as a burnt offering to this Lord you *follow, who has given you nothing in return. You don't even have any good meat to eat. That stag would make many meals for you."*

Kief reached down at his sack and felt the two rabbits Lesh had given him. He was thinking about them, how he would only get two or three meals at the most from them. The only other food in the house was the bag of oats and bag of wheat he had stored in the back. However, the meat of the stag would certainly fill his belly and taste better.

Before he spoke, the one calling himself Dagon spoke instead. "You could give the two rabbits as an offering, and still keep in good order with your Lord. That way, you could have more food to live on until you can make another kill. Your Lord will not mind the small offering this one time."

Kief turned toward the meat of the stag and felt hunger stir in his stomach. He was hungry, and stag would taste good about now. Perhaps just this one time the Lord would accept not only one rabbit, like others whom he had known had offered, but two rabbits. "Of course your Lord will accept the two rabbits...." the voice of the shadowed figure fell away, as Kief turned back to see nothing but the back wall. Yes, he thought to himself, the Lord would accept the rabbits. The Lord would understand.

He put the sack of rabbits on the table out of the way and began to prepare the stag for his meals. When it was ready, he put one piece in a pot to cook for his supper and stored the rest before turning his attention back to the rabbits.

The day came when the people of Janish were to offer their best to the Lord. The temple where the offerings were to be placed sat on the hill overlooking the village. Steps of rock had been set into the path leading up to the temple courtyard. The courtyard was small, but the temple itself was just a small building, no bigger than a house. It was only used for the offerings that were given to the Lord every week. Men lined up along the path with their offerings, as their families, if they had families, stood off of the bottom of the stair path in solemn prayer, as was their way.

Kief stood halfway along the path, watching Lesh preparing to enter the temple with his offering. He was supposed to meet him before heading up, but he was purposely late so that Lesh would not see his offering of rabbits he had prepared. He watched Lesh nod to the White Seraph standing at the door of the temple. A few moments later, Lesh came out and made his way to the path on the side, which led back down to the village. Kief was trying to think of an excuse of what to tell him later about why he was late.

The rabbits were contained in a burlap bag, wrapped carefully and carried in his arms like a small child. Kief slowly made his way up, and when it was his time, he too gave the nod to the White Seraph before he entered. Once inside, he found an empty place, and unwrapped his offering and laid it on the site he had picked. Kief poured the oil, which was there for that purpose, over his offering and knelt to say a prayer to the Lord. Then he stood and left the same way as he had seen Lesh do.

He saw Lesh standing with his family, and when Lesh noticed Kief both nodded at one another and smiled. No words were supposed to be spoken until the Lord took the offering. When the last man left the temple and had made his way down to the others, the entire village: man, woman, and child, knelt on their knees and prayed. A loud boom sounded in the sky, and Keif peeked and watched the clouds part as a column of fire shot down into the temple. Moments later, it was over. A few moments after that, the people of the village stood back up and began to head home. Kief turned and started home. On his way, he watched as the others were preparing for the village feast in the square as was custom. The village feast was a time of fellowship among people, sharing food and telling good stories with one another. Kief continued to his home and prepared a meal just for himself, sat down, and began to eat. Outside, he could hear the prayer of grace and blessings for the food they were about to receive. Then they were eating.

As he was finishing up, he looked up and saw the White

Seraph standing over him in his bright, pure-white hooded cloak. Kief felt his face turn pale. "Why are you not out fellowshipping with the others? Could it be that you have not given the best of your weekly spoils to the Lord? Has he not provided for you, given you enough food for your stomach, given you all you need?"

Kief just stammered. The White Seraph continued. "The Lord has not accepted your offering, for it was not your spoil that you gave. Lesh has given the rabbits for your food to eat, and the kill of the stag was yours to give to the Lord. Lesh has received double the blessings. If you would only obey the Laws of the Lord, the Laws given to the people of Gal-Gilead, you too would have the many blessings of the Lord."

He vanished, and on the table were the two rabbits he had prepared for his offering. Kief just stood and looked out of the window watching the others eating. He didn't know how to feel. He just felt numb.

"It does make you angry, doesn't it?" he heard a voice behind him say. It was the shadowed figure. "Look at your best friend out there. He gets double the blessings while you get nothing. It seems that this Lord of yours is selfish, in not accepting your offerings."

"But we are supposed to give the Lord the best," Kief replied. "And I did not do that."

"But you have to eat," Dagon answered, his form still looking *like he was part of the wind. "You may not get a kill this next week. You might not eat for weeks, and this meat you have will last a good while and give you a chance to fill your stomach."*

Kief kept watching Lesh, sitting there with his wife and his child, laughing in fellowship with the other villagers. Dagon moved closer behind him. "Look at him. He has forgotten all about you. He doesn't care about you. He already has everything you want, and now he has taken your blessings. He probably knew you would lose your blessings, which is why he gave you those rabbits in the first place. He has a healthy young son, and a beautiful wife, which you liked when you were younger, did you not?"

"I had a crush on her, yes. However, Lesh married her, and she is his now. I must look for another one. One day, I will marry."

"Or if Lesh had an accident while hunting and died, you would have that chance again. That chance for his blessing." The shadowy figure faded. It would be nice, he thought, to have what Lesh had. Lesh was a great hunter, and could never have a hunting accident. Not without help.

Kief Dan shook the thoughts of this out of his mind in a sudden feeling of guilt. Tomorrow they would go hunting, and everything would be as before.

It was early morning when Kief and Lesh met in the square of the village, ready to hunt, as they always did. "Missed you at the village dinner," Lesh said to him as he walked up, carrying his bow.

Kief brushed it off like it was something simple. He knew why he didn't go, but he wasn't going to let on to his friend what it was. So Kief lied. "I wasn't feeling too good," he said. "But I feel better now. I might get a good kill today."

Lesh smiled. "I hope so. Let's go." They headed out of the village, heading in a different direction this time. Today was a good day to head northeast toward the mountains.

It took nearly an hour through woods before they started heading up. They fixed up one of their blinds and sat and waited. Hours passed before a stag appeared. It was walking several feet away and stopped to eat some of the foliage that grew near a giant oak. "You want this one?" he asked Kief.

"You go first this time. Maybe you'll miss, and I'll get the save." He got the arrow and prepared for the kill, in case Lesh missed.

Lesh stood quietly over the brush and drew back his bow, and the arrow released, meeting its mark in the stag's neck. The beast fell where it ate. "Should have taken it," he smiled as he walked out from behind the blind and headed toward his kill. He knelt down and examined the stag.

From where the stag came, Kief heard a rustling and watched another stag step out into the opening. It huffed through its nostrils and stared at Lesh. Kief pulled the arrow back on the bow aiming it at the new animal, just as it began to run toward his friend. The aim of the bolt was focused on the stag's head as it charged, and he was ready to release it when a familiar voice whispered into his ear.

"Not yet."

Kief held back and watched as the stag bolted straight into Lesh, just as he turned. Lesh rolled under the hooves and over the kill. The stag kept running and disappeared into the trees. Kief moved quickly to his friend and saw the blood on his chest, which was being spat up from his mouth. Lesh was still alive. "Help me, Kief."

He reached down to help him, then saw Lesh's eyes widen. Behind him, Kief heard the voice again. "This is your accident. The moment you have been waiting for."

He turned around to see the Dark Seraph standing there, then he looked down at Lesh. Lesh shook his head, choking in fear at what he saw. With the shadowy figure of the Dark Seraph speaking to his friend, he knew something was wrong.

The shadowy figure spoke. "With this kill, you could have everything you ever wanted; the wife, the child, the lifestyle." Kief looked back down at his friend, and he knew Lesh knew. The figure continued, "No one would ever be the wiser. You would be the comforter to his wife, the father to his son, and a hero to the people. He cannot be healed. Take the rock and end his misery."

He looked down into his hand and saw it cupped a sharp rock. Looking back at his fallen comrade, he watched the fear in Lesh's widening eyes as he lifted the rock over his head. The Dark Seraph leaned in to whisper in his ear. "Do it."

At that moment, Keif felt his raised arm, gripping the rock, come down hard on his friend's head. Lesh was silent from then on. Kief turned, and the shadowy figure was gone. In the distance, he saw two other figures watching him.

Two more hunters from his village had witnessed his actions, and Kief knew what would happen then. The two called his name, and Kief stood up, and ran the opposite way, heading upward toward the mountain top. What he was going to do, he didn't know. Keif was going to get nothing but death back to Janish. He felt sick to his stomach, his legs only stopped when he knew he was too far away to be followed. What seemed like hours later, Kief finally found a cave near the mountain top, where he went in and hid. He laid down in the dirt floor of the cave and fell asleep.

"Kief Dan."

Kief's eyes opened slowly. He thought he heard someone calling him. He continued to hold silent. Maybe it was a dream.

"Kief Dan."

He had heard it this time, and a strange fear came over him. He still held silent.

The voice became slightly more demanding. "Kief Dan. Come forth from the cave."

"I'm scared," Kief replied.

"Come forth from the cave. You cannot hide from the Lord."

Kief obeyed then, for he knew it was the White Seraph. It was dusk outside when he walked out, and most of the light seemed to be coming from the White Seraph. His eyes began to water.

"You have committed evil on the people of your village, and against a man, you called a friend. You have broken one of the laws of the Lord your God. Murder is evil. Why did you do this?"

Kief looked down, ashamed. His throat was dry and began to tighten as he spoke. "I was tempted by the shadowed man."

"The murder was still in your hand. It was your choice."

A bit of anger came over him. "All my life I have been looked down on by the people of the village. I got nothing while everyone got everything they wanted."

"Did you not trust God to do for you what He has done for them."

There was no answer from Kief. He had no rebuttal.

The White Seraph then spoke after a moment. "You are banished from Gal-Gilead forever, never to return. You will leave by the mountain pass, and it will be closed to you."

"I'm scared," was his reply. "I don't want to die out in the wilderness."

The White Seraph said, "You will not die from an animal nor in the wilderness. You will die by the hand of another, as your friend has died by your hands."

Kief felt a little spark of relief. He dried his eyes and obeyed, walking down the mountain, finding his way to the pass that would lead him away from the home he had always known. Keif didn't know what he was going to do, and he didn't know what was out there. He knew he would have to prove himself no matter what he did.

Nicolea heard Jon calling him. He gathered his things and the things Lenok had given him, placed them in his satchel, and left.

CHAPTER EIGHT
Spaceflight

The mist began to roll onto the shores of Illosha as they approached the waiting boatman. Jon could feel the wetness of the mist on his skin as he stepped into the boat. He looked down, seeing Nicolea sitting in the front, and Lenok behind him with his pack and staff. Once they were aboard Rosha pushed the boat into the water with his oar and began steering the boat ahead. The further out they went, the thicker the mist became.

"Why is the mist this bad?" Jon asked. "It didn't last this long on the way in."

"You have enemies on the shore," Rosha said. "The mist will protect you as it protects the island."

When the boat slid onto the sands of the shore Jon

stepped out, following Nicolea and Lenok as a corridor of clarity led them to the stealth ship that they had left on the beach. As they walked along the cleared path Jon could see just within the mist. Bodies were visible on the ground and he wondered if they were dead.

"They're asleep," said Lenok, as if reading his mind. "They are your enemies and seek to do evil. We have a purpose, which is why we are being protected."

Behind them, the boat had already left the shore and was probably heading back to Illosha. Soon they had made their way onto the ship and had lifted off-world, going to see Thermonte Electrik.

When Bjorn Chelli opened his eyes, the first thing he noticed was that the ship was not there. He wanted to be angry, but he had heard of the mysteriousness of the island. It would have been easier on the mission if he had at least captured the men who had come from the island, but it wasn't necessary.

He stood up and shouted to his men to get up and get ready to move out. They all gathered themselves up out of their confused stupor. He found Jenson and took him aside.

"You and the Mage stay here just in case they return."

Jenson nodded. "You got it."

Within the hour Bjorn and his men were on their way back to Drakoon.

Once in space and en route to Chotis, Jon tried to contact Synoa Station and let them know what had transpired. After many tries, he gave up. There was no answer. He looked up at Nicolea and said, "No one is answering. You think they are alright?"

It was Lenok who answered him. "They are safe. Your Admiral Shepherd has informed them of the situation. They have gone elsewhere."

"How do you know these things?" Jon asked.

Lenok smiled at him. "How do I know the things I do?" He answered with a question. Then to Nicolea, who had been flying the ship, he asked, "How long before we get to this Mr. Electrik?"

"About twelve hours."

Lenok stood up out of the seat he had been occupying and slowly walked into the corridor. "I will be somewhere in quiet communion," he said. Then he left.

Thermonte Electrik sat in his chair in his den as he usually did these days, drinking a drink he shouldn't be drinking, waiting on someone he wasn't sure was coming to see him. Soshiana walked into the room, standing just inside, and Thermonte looked over at her with half-drunken eyes. "Well?" he said, not expecting anything from her. It had been almost a week, probably more than a week, since he had heard from Agent Vega.

"Better sober up," Soshiana replied. "They just entered the system."

Thermonte straightened up. He laid his drink on the table and jerked up his shirt sleeve. "Give me a boost," he ordered his bio-tek. She walked over to him, placing her right thumb on his arm, and shot in a booster. Thermonte was suddenly sober.

He stood up, straightening his clothes. "Let's go prepare for the welcome. Is the Chimera ready for lift-off?"

"I believe so. Should I go and get it ready to leave?" Soshiana asked him.

"No, not yet," he answered back. "We'll go down together when they get here. I don't want anyone thinking I'm doing something crooked."

Mr. Electrik moved to the facilities that were located off to the side of the den to finish fixing himself into a proper state. Soshiana took her to leave, and when there was a knock at the door, she answered it. She recognized Jon Vega and Nicolea Dan, but not the third man. This man wearing old robes and carrying a staff was very odd to her. She said nothing.

Instead, she led them into the den where Thermonte Electrik stood at the large bay windows looking out onto the mountain-surrounded lake. He was always one to act like he was in control of everything, even in this instance. He turned around and smiled at them. "Welcome back, Agent Vega." He nodded toward Nicolea and said, "And you, Mr. Dan."

He noticed the third man just as Soshiana had done. "Who is your friend?" he asked.

It was Lenok who introduced himself. "I am Lenok, son of Lesh, from the Isle of Illosha on the world of Bel Terra."

Smiling a strange smile, Thermonte stared at him. His eyes moved around the man and settled on the small, strange carvings on his staff. He lifted his hand, pointing his finger as if he had just figured out something no one else had yet figured out. "I have heard rumors."

"Rumors about what?" Jon asked him, still unwilling to trust or even like him.

Ignoring Jon, Thermonte kept staring at Lenok. "You

are one of those immortal or celestial people. Am I right?"

Lenok laughed then. "Not at all. Neither immortal or from the celestial realm, from your point of view. At least I am not one yet. I am known as a Prophet Warrior. I am here to help you fight the aliens, as you call them. I am anxious to see this water in space, as you called it, wasn't it?"

"Ah, yes, the water in space," Thermonte repeated. "You will see it, but it will take two years. First, we need to take a trip to Dragmar."

"Why is that?" It was Lenok who had asked. He seemed more curious than anything. He hadn't been in the fully physical world for a long time.

Thermonte smiled, feeling somewhat pleased with himself for what he was going to reveal. "There is a faster-than-light ship, constructed by Dr. Phaleg."

"Phaleg?" Lenok asked. "I've heard that name before."

Jon wasn't there for chit chat. The sooner he got this done, the better. He wanted to put Mr. Electrik behind bars. His thoughts on him were nothing short of hate.

It was Nicolea who brought up the notion of getting started. "So," he had begun, "when do we get to leave for this Dragmar?"

"Soshiana, I believe you told me the Chimera is ready?" Soshiana nodded in reply. He continued, "Then let us retire to my yacht. It will only take us about a week to get there."

Leading the way was Soshiana, then Thermonte, who seemed to be talking on and on about things that Jon didn't think mattered to anyone. But at least they were on their way. The staircase led far down into the cliffside the house sat on before finally entering the bay where the ship was docked. Inside sat the largest yacht-class ship Jon had ever seen.

It was a shiny silver trimmed in a dull yellow. It was the kind of yacht that could float within the atmosphere of a world and then cover the decks and head into space. Jon thought it was likely bigger than his apartment on Tiere.

Soshiana assigned each one their private room, then made her way onto the bridge of the yacht. As everyone settled in the stateroom located above the private quarters, Soshiana controlled the ship herself with relative ease.

Once in space and heading toward Dragmar, Soshiana was able to serve dinner in the side parlor of the stateroom. The meal, though simply prepared, was far better than the guests were used to eating, and the conversation slowed as everyone ate his fill. Jon had been quiet the entire time, barely speaking at any length. He found that his mind began to wander.

He began to wonder about the past, the island of Illosha, and how fantastic it had seemed. So unreal, he thought it was in his mind. He heard the conversation of the others, but they seemed distant, far off. Lenok seemed to be interested in the criminal's discussion and had asked him many questions, which seemed to please Mr. Electrik and bolster his pride.

Nicolea seemed more interested in the world surrounding Lenok, his past, his teachings, every word he spoke. Jon had noticed, too, his intense interest in the initial introduction between Lenok and Thermonte.

Nicolea may have been fully involved in the conversation, but he was also aware of Jon's distance. He figured he might ask him what was on his mind later, when there wasn't so much going on.

Jon had made his way to the couch, which was facing the large window looking out onto the passing stars. It always looked like the stars were passing you, instead of you passing the stars, thought Jon. Unlike ground travel, space flight lacked the right noise and feel to remind you that you were in fact the one moving. Soon, he was tuning everyone else out, and thinking more about the things of his past, while watching the motion of the stars.

When he thought of Thermonte speaking about the waters in space, then seeing the waters dislocated between the two trees on Illosha, it almost made him believe in the strange and spirited things. Lenok had told him that he would not be able to go entirely through the water, for his flesh would die. Only the spirit and soul could make the long journey, which in that form, was not a long journey at that. Like a blink of an eye, he remembered Lenok saying. In fact, he had just mentioned it to the group at the table just now. They had been speaking about the waters that Thermonte had mentioned.

Jon averted his attention away from the people and resumed watching the stars. He loved being in space, and the beauty of the stars against the black curtain. Light piercing the dark was one thought that had crossed his mind. He honestly did not know what to make of all this.

"You're quiet," Nicolea said.

Jon didn't realize Nicolea was sitting next to him, or when he had even sat down. "Just keeping to my own mind. I find Mr. Electrik reprehensible. I just can't stand him. Why are we even entertaining this thought? You know it's probably a trap."

Nicolea shrugged. "I don't know him like you do. I've never had dealings with him, working for the Federation. But if it is a trap, why just us?"

"Maybe he was a part of this invasion all along," Jon suggested. "They weakened our forces and defense, and we're just in the way of the overall plan."

"Perhaps," Nicolea agreed, but he wasn't too sure. He knew there must be something on a much bigger scale going on here. He didn't know exactly what, but they would all find out soon.

As to Mr. Electrik being a part of all this, he found that the crime lord was frustrated and concerned about what was happening. Now, whether he was a part of it before and had gotten removed from it by the enemy, he had no idea. That was a possibility. "I think I am going to turn in and do some reading before I go to sleep."

Jon watched his friend stand up. "Let me guess. Lenok gave you more scrolls to read."

Nicolea smiled. "Yea, he did. I'm learning quite a bit

about my past, where I came from. Maybe you should ask him about some scrolls about your own past. I'm sure he might be able to come up with something."

"That's alright," he replied. "I have my reservations about him, too."

Nicolea just smiled and walked out of the room. His plans tonight included reading from the second scroll about his ancient heritage.

This left Jon alone again. He wished he could have gotten in touch with Synoa Station and the president. Lieutenant Shane would take his report back with the ship, but he wondered if they were okay and what had happened to them. Lenok seemed to know, but that was another story. He trusted this Lenok more than he trusted Mr. Electrik. Things just didn't seem right to him.

Finally, he yawned, and he stood up and made his way to his room. His mind needed a rest, and perhaps he could start fresh in the morning.

CHAPTER NINE

Second Scroll of Dan

Lenok, son of Lesh, from the village of Janis in the region of Gal-Gilead, was under the tutelage of the priest there. When Lesh had been killed by Kief Dan, the White Seraph had comforted Sareen, his wife. In gratitude, she had dedicated her unborn child to the Lord of Light, and so, as promised, at the age of five Lenok entered the wardship of the priesthood.

The White Seraph came to Lenok during his daily morning meditation. He was seven. "Son of Lesh, open your eyes."

Lenok opened his eyes and saw the lighted, shimmering figure before him. "Do you know who I am?" the figure asked. Lenok nodded, saying nothing. The White Seraph continued. "Your mother, Sareen, is ill. Go to your home and escort her to the white sands of Northshire, beyond the Mountain Road. There she will find peace and you will find comfort."

Three days later, Lenok took his mother on the week-long journey to the white sands on the edge of the North Sea. There they met a man, robed in white, standing near a small boat. "I am Rosha. They are waiting for both of you."

Rosha held his hand out toward the boat, and mother and son both understood. Sareen knew what was waiting. When the White Seraph had comforted her after her husband had been killed, he had said, "Worry not, for your husband was a righteous man, and he walks beyond this world. The son you carry in your womb will also be a righteous man and will become a shepherd over his people."

Mother and son sat in the boat and Rosha moved it away from the shore. There was a sudden mist and it surrounded them and they moved ahead.

Kief Dan had been living in New Galmesh, the royal city of Connacht, on the eastern border of the clear blue expanse of the Halcyon Sea. He had become involved with a woman named Nathara, the daughter of King Alic of Connacht. It was through her insistence that Kief Dan had become a member of the secret cult of Dagon.

Dagon appeared as a shadowy figure that was known to many as the Dark Seraph. It had been twenty years since the White

Seraph banished him from Gal-Gilead, beyond the mountain pass. Once again, Dagon appeared to Kief Dan. He was alone when he heard Dagon's voice.

"You have done well for yourself, Kief Dan. Welcome to the royal city. How would you like to rule this world?"

Kief looked up. "Why should I listen to you now? You sold me out to my own people."

"Those who suffer are rewarded with treasures."

"What treasure?"

"You are in love with the king's daughter. She is in love with you. Marry her, and you will be king. You will have power beyond your imagination."

After a moment of silence, Kief spoke again. "What do you get out of this, Dagon?"

"I'm only here to help you achieve your greatness. You make me god of Connacht. It's all your rule, and I only get worshipped."

More silence, before the Dark Seraph spoke again. "Nathara is a true believer. Elevating me to my rightful place as god of the land, you will make her yours forever. She is most beautiful."

"So what's Dagon the god of?" he asked.

"Pleasure and prosperity."

The shadowy figure seemed to fade then, and Kief was alone. Things were looking up for him. In fact, things were good. Maybe he should ask Nathara to marry him. And then, when the king passed on, he would be king. It was a thought.

Within the year he married the princess and became the well-received Prince of New Galmesh, Prince of Connacht. Around the city the people rejoiced at the union of Prince Kief and Princess Nathara. There was no group that rejoiced more than the mass calling themselves the Shadows of Dagon. Nathara was one of those in that shadow.

Three months later King Alic became ill and bed-ridden. Only the Princess was allowed to visit him. He had become worried, because the idols of Dagon had slowly been appearing around the city. She was the only person he would trust to rid the city of those idols. He had brought her up in the ways of the one true God. He did not trust her husband, because he knew little about him. He had played the part of a great young man, but King Alic hadn't known him long enough to be sure. When you were king, people had a habit of not showing their true selves to you. He did not tell his fears to Nathara, and she just smiled and agreed with him, telling him everything would be fine.

The day the king died a statue of Dagon was erected in the palace courtyard. It was decreed that he would now be worshipped by all peoples in New Galmesh. For twenty years the Palace grew in wealth and the city grew into unrighteousness.

Jerod Dan was walking the streets of New Galmesh looking for the followers of the White Seraph. The son of King Kief and

Queen Nathara, he had been given authority to find the agitators against Dagon. He had killed many in the two years he had been doing this, and he was good at it. He was known for being cruel, and no one got in his way. In fact, the people who worshipped Dagon cheered him on.

He was walking down one of the back alleyways leading to the home of a woman that was known to go against Dagon worshippers when he was struck down by a massive light. He fell to his knees and became blind, hearing only a voice in front of him. "Why are you persecuting the believers of the one true God?"

"Dagon is the god," he replied.

"Dagon is a lie. You worship a lie."

Jerod's eyes began to receive their vision back. "Who are you that you can do this to a man in daylight?"

"I am but a messenger of the one true God. I am here to tell you that you still have a choice. A choice to serve the truth."

When his eyes opened, he saw the White Seraph standing in front of him, and he new it was the truth. No one had seen the White Seraph in years. According to the priests of Dagon, the White Seraph had long since stopped appearing to man.

"What will you have me do now?"

"Find the woman you were to find, she is waiting to take you south beyond Connacht. There you will be shown the ways of the *true God, and you will spread the word of Him."*

Jerod stood up and went his way, and found the woman, whose name was Bea. She took him out of the city at night and was not seen again. This was twenty years to the day from his birth, which was one year after Kief had become King.

One year passed, and nothing in New Galmesh had changed. Lenok, the son of Lesh, stood on the northern shore, having been brought over from Illosha by the boatman. He was older now than when he was brought there by his mother twenty two years ago. He stood there dressed in the dark olive robes of a Prophet Warrior and a dark brown cloak to cover the fact. His long black hair was cropped around his face within the hood, and his beard was starting to show the need for a trim. There was purpose in this. There was always purpose when a Prophet Warrior stood on the shores of Northshire.

His staff was made of amberwood, the strongest wood in Connacht, found only on the island of Illosha. "Do you know what you are here to do?"

Lenok turned to his left, where the White Seraph was shimmering next to him. "You will travel to New Galmesh to the house of Boran. He will lead you to the courtyard of the royal palace, where you will confront Kief during the festival of Dagon. Beware of the shadows around him, for they will deceive you with their words."

"Why me?" It was Lenok's only reply.

"There is history between your family and his. You will tell him who you are and then warn him of his evil ways. You will tell him to destroy the idols of Dagon."

Lenok nodded. "I understand. I hope I am ready."

"The Lord chose you for this task," the White Seraph told him. "It must be taken care of, before the darkness overtakes the world and the hearts of mankind."

The White Seraph faded into the sunlight. Lenok took hold of his amberwood staff and began his slow journey into the city of New Galmesh. There he rested and filled his belly with food and meditated until the morning of the festival.

Boran was a man of faith of the true Lord God. He taught the ways of the Lord God in secret away from the prying eyes of the priests and the so-called judges of Dagon. They were the ones in charge of hunting down those like Boran.

The morning of the festival Boran led Lenok, dressed in his robes and cloak, through the crowd in the city streets. All the people were making their way toward the palace courtyard. There each citizen, or family, was to make their pledge to Dagon and the royal family. On the front veranda of the palace sat the twin thrones of the king and queen. From there they watched as the people came and pledged their life to them, and then turned and did the same to the idol of Dagon. As Lenok followed Boran into the line, he placed his hand on his shoulder.

"You and the others stand outside the courtyard. This is not for you."

Boran nodded and turned and left, making eye contact with a few friends as he did so. Lenok gripped his staff with both hands and continued to move forward.

Finally at the head of the line, he stepped in front of the king and queen of New Galmesh, both hands grasping his staff, his head bowed. He looked like an obedient citizen, but he was praying to the Lord God to calm his own fear.

"What does this citizen of New Galmesh and follower of Dagon have to pledge to this royal house and his god Dagon?" It was the voice of Kief Dan.

Lenok answered. "I am not a citizen of New Galmesh, nor am I a follower of your false god."

Anger appeared in the the king's voice. "Then just who are you to betray the sanctity of Dagon?" His voice was loud and commanding. The queen's head was held high. Silence fell across the people in the courtyard.

Lenok looked up. Behind the thrones stood the priests of Dagon, and looking around, he saw the judges of Dagon step out into the open. The people had moved back on the other side of the giant statue of the false god.

"I am Lenok, son of Lesh." He pointed to the king. "You, Kief Dan, have fallen into the shadows of darkness and evil and conspired with the Dark Seraph to lead the people into evil."

The king stood in anger. "I am the king of Connacht. You will not speak to me in that manner, young Lenok. You will not destroy all we have worked for."

"You are an evil man. Confess now, and repent, or feel the wrath of the Lord of Light, the one true God."

Kief was shouting now. "I will confess nothing, blasphemer!"

Lenok threw off his cloak and gripped his staff again. "I was sent by the Lord God as His Prophet Warrior to bring justice back to Connacht and His people."

With that, the judges of Dagon began to move in toward him. Lenok raised his staff and jolted it to the ground. A strong wave of wind emanated from the staff and the judges fell to the ground and died. Then he pointed at the royal family. "Repent now, King Kief Dan and Queen Nathara, and end this wickedness. Destroy the idols of Dagon."

Kief hesitated. He remembered the words of the White Seraph many years ago, and what the Dark Seraph had only done for himself. His mind put it in order.

Next to him, Queen Nathara stood watching. Behind her, she felt the presence of the shadowed man. He whispered to her. "He will betray you. You must kill him. I will save you. Run to the south and to the fields of Drakoon. There is a tree with large roots. Hide within those roots. I will save you."

The presence was gone.

Nathara reached for the ceremonial dagger at her side. She turned to the priests behind her. "Kill that man!" she shouted, pointing to the Prophet Warrior.

As the priests moved in, sacrificial knives in their hands, Nathara took the pin and shoved it deep into her king's neck. Kief's eyes widened when he heard her voice. "You betrayed Dagon."

The priests of Dagon charged toward Lenok. Lenok took his staff and fought them off. These men were true believers of Dagon, and they knew that they would be rewarded by the queen herself. But their attack failed as quickly as it had begun, and as each one fell, the idol of Dagon began to crumble.

When the fight was over, Lenok turned back to see Kief dead in front of the throne, blood pouring from his neck. King Kief Dan was dead, and was killed by the hand of another. One he loved.

Lenok turned toward the idol then and struck the staff on the ground three times. A bolt of lightning came from the skies and devoured the remains of the idol of Dagon, and all the idols of Dagon within the city.

Darkness fell away from the city, and the people suddenly

realized what they had been doing. They had been doing it willingly, and they fell to their faces and repented in front of the Prophet Warrior. Lenok felt the White Seraph next to him.

"You must stay for a time and choose a new king. When you see him, you will know. This land will heal."

Nathara stood in the fields of Drakoon, in front of the tree with the giant roots. A figure stood there all in black, and his face was beautiful. She felt love for this man.

He spoke. "Come Nathara, your destiny is waiting for you here, with me." She walked closer and they disappeared into the roots.

CHAPTER TEN
World Of Shadows

The world of Dragmar was mostly uninhabited, with only the station that Thermonte had described providing any population. It was smaller than Jon had expected. The Chimera entered the atmosphere of the small planet, jerking from side to side as it encountered the rough winds.

They all stood on the small bridge watching as Soshiana guided the yacht towards the surface, expertly compensating for the strong winds. Soon the ship was closing in on the facility, slowing down just above the building. Soshiana transmitted some codes, and the roof opened up, sliding to the side. In the distance ahead of them, a storm was brewing. The atmosphere gave off a brown-orange light. Bolts of bright orange lightning slapped the ground, coming closer. As the yacht began to lower into the building, those on the bridge didn't seem to notice as the winds became even stronger.

Once inside, the ship docked, and the doors closed. When they stepped off the ship, the sounds of the storm could not be heard. "Welcome to Dragmar," Mr. Electrik stated. "I know the world isn't much, but this facility is amazing. It is larger than a small village."

"So where is this faster-than-light ship you're so proud of?" Jon asked him.

Thermonte smiled. He knew Jon did not trust him and did not like him. "Jon, can we not move past this? You need to try and learn to trust me."

Jon just looked at him. "You're a criminal. Just another criminal. Sometimes a cop needs to work with the low-life to get to the bigger fish in the organization. That's what I'm doing here. So, where is this ship?"

"That hurt, Jon." Thermonte looked around, walking around the group. "You are standing on the ship."

He was quiet for a moment, letting his words sink in. Lenok walked up with his staff, his satchel around his back. "Well then, let's get this FTL ship moving. We have two years of travel to get through."

They all agreed, and followed Soshiana, who seemed to be the only one who knew where things were, and how things worked. Even Nicolea wondered if Thermonte had ever been here before. He had claimed he had, but there was reason for doubt.

The group followed Soshiana, looking at the ship while she checked the provisions and fuel. Afterward she showed them all to where the sleeping pods were, then they made their way to the bridge. Again, Soshiana was the pilot of this ship, only asking Nicolea to help navigate. The ship, which was simply dubbed the FTL, broke away from its moorings.

The ship had not been the whole facility, but merely a part of it. The FTL was shaped like a shortened lower-case "t," with the large faster-than-light engines on the ends of the outstretched arms. Another set of normal engines were at the back. Special shielding could be activated to cover the viewports for faster-than-light travel.

The atmospheric storm had moved on, making it easier to lift up above the ground and make their way off-world. Within minutes, the larger ship was in space. Soshiana maneuvered the FTL into position using the coordinates her boss had given her earlier, and the ship quickly moved into light speed. The two massive engines on the ends of the arms of the ship began to light up, with a bright white light pouring out of their rear, and with a loud internal-sounding boom, the ship made the jump into faster-than-light.

Another boom could be heard, and Jon and the others suddenly felt more speed. It was an odd sensation. Even as they made their way to the sleeping pods, they could all feel the moving sensation in space.

Nicolea, Jon, and Mr. Electrik each entered one of the sleeping pods in the room. Jon made sure Thermonte was in one before he himself submitted to being put to sleep for two years. Before Nicolea went down, he said a short prayer to the Lord of Light, then climbed into the pod to sleep. Soshiana, whose bio-tek body would sustain her through the two years, remained awake to monitor the ship. Lenok also did not take the sleep. It actually made Jon feel more comfortable knowing he was not sleeping.

Lenok was given his own small cabin near the rear of the ship, and there he stayed for most of the trip, reading the scrolls and praying. Soshiana rarely saw him. Usually it was when he emerged to get water and something to eat. Luckily, Mr. Electrik had plenty of food on the ship. He had packed well.

Now and then he would check on the sleeping crew and make sure everyone was doing fine. Occasionally Soshiana saw him on the bridge, as he came to check on her. She figured he just needed someone to talk to, which was true, but only to an extent. Then he would disappear back into his cabin and continue his prayers and reading.

Two years later.

Unknown space surrounded the FTL ship as it glided smoothly across the star-filled dark glass. Nicolea Dan, now sporting a short beard and slightly longer hair, walked onto the bridge. He came to a stop behind Soshiana, who was piloting the giant craft.

"I see we jumped back into normal space," Nicolea commented, staring out into the great creation.

"We came back into real space about an hour ago," she replied. "I'm running us along the coordinate path given me by Thermonte. We should be at our destination soon."

"Should we go ahead and wake the others?"

"I have already initiated the codes to the sleeping pods to awaken the others. You simply responded more quickly." She never took her hands or eyes off the instruments on the panel.

It was several hours later when the other two came in. First was Jon, stumbling in and looking like he was still waking up. Then came Mr. Electrik, spilling out a speech about the beauty of space and the stars and such. After everyone was awake Lenok joined them, leaning on his staff, with his satchel strapped across his chest.

He looked at Nicolea and stopped. "You're starting to look the part," Lenok said to him. "How was the trip?"

Nicolea smiled back at him. "Extraordinarily peaceful."

The ship came to a stop. "There it is," Soshiana reported.

Everyone looked out past the viewport into the sea of stars. There it was. A liquid wall of dark water. The water wasn't actually dark, but it reflected the darkness around it. Jon thought back to the water doorway he saw on Illosha. This one seemed to extend in all directions.

"Fire a torpedo into it," Thermonte told her.

Before anyone could protest, Soshiana had loaded a torpedo and had fired it straight into the water. The projectile entered the water, causing a ripple effect. No explosion took place. No big splash. Nothing.

"Well, that sure was an interesting experiment," Lenok said. Then one of the lights reflecting on the water wall caught their eye. This light, from the system's sun, had a hole in it where a planet cast its shadow against the wall.

Soshiana understood the next part without being told. She scanned the planet and acknowledged what the others felt. "There seems to be life below on the world. Sending signals to the surface."

"Ask for Andrelus Pan," Thermonte told her. "Tell them who I am."

A few moments passed, then a voice came over the comms. "Thermonte Electrik, welcome to Khair Din, the world of shadows."

"Who am I talking to?" Mr. Electrik asked.

"I am Andrelus Pan. You did ask for me, did you not?"

Jon was watching the gangster's face and was seeing

that perhaps Thermonte was telling the truth. It seemed that it started out being Thermonte's project to do whatever, but it was taken over by this Andrelus Pan. He could see the anger in Thermonte's face.

Mr. Electrik's next statement confirmed what Jon had thought. "Why was I cut out of this? Why did you throw me away? I was promised."

Then there was a voice Mr. Electrik seemed to know. "Mr. Electrik," said the voice, "this is Doctor Phaleg. Why don't you come on down and we'll talk. And bring your friends with you."

Jon didn't trust this voice, nor did Nicolea or any of the others. It was Lenok who suggested that they prepare for battle before going down. They all agreed at once. They gathered together all the weapons they had stored on board and made their way to the shuttle bay. There was a standard transport shuttle sitting alone in the hanger.

Soshiana got behind the controls. "There is a small group of buildings near what seems to be mountains of some kind. That is where the communications came from."

Jon and Nicolea, who were used to operating such as this, took charge. Jon actually took control, and Nicolea agreed with his operation. They would land outside the group of buildings and make their way carefully in. They would be cautious, checking every angle, every corner, and every possibility. The only one not carrying a weapon was Lenok. Lenok had left his satchel in his cabin, but he carried his staff. It was the only defense he had.

Mr. Electrik had a handheld tucked in the front of his pants, which was awkward to him, since he also wore an armored military vest. In his hands he carried a standard blast rifle with a grenade launcher. He wasn't fully unaware of how to use weapons. Both Jon and Nicolea looked like true military fighters, carrying multiple weapons and ammunition, among other devices a soldier would carry.

Soshiana just brought herself. She was her own weapon.

The shuttle lifted off and, with the shuttle's controls linked to the ship, the bay doors opened and the shuttle left, heading down to the planet below.

Khair Din was a small world compared to others that were inhabited, even those that were colony worlds. The red sun gave the world's atmosphere a somewhat red haze, and the world looked devastated. Strong winds blew across the red-hazed frontier so hard that the shuttle rocked against the turbulent descent. At one point, Lenok was thrown against the opposite hull of the ship, having forgot that he needed to be strapped in. He was a bit embarrassed, but okay.

After landing, Soshiana took a reading of the air outside the shuttle. "There is a bubble of pure oxygen surrounding the buildings, but we'll need oxygen masks outside the ship until we get there," reported Soshiana, moving to the back with the rest and opening up a lockbox on the wall.

There were five transparent face masks connected directly to an oxygen converter on the front. Each member took one, and opening the back of the shuttle, they all moved out, not sure what they would find.

Yellow streaks of lightning shot horizontally across the red sky, momentarily brightening up the surrounding environment. Jon took point, moving in quick militia style toward the buildings. Everyone moved, or tried to move, quickly behind him, with Nicolea pulling up the rear. Mr. Electrik was the only one who seemed to fall behind, causing them to move slower. The yellow lightning flashed across the sky every now and again, sometimes followed by thunder that echoed strangely off the mountains. It was so loud at times that it almost left a ringing in their ears.

Once they moved into the bubble, it was Soshiana that pulled off her mask first, strapping it to her belt. Everyone followed suit. "There is no one here," Mr. Electric said, looking around the area.

"They're here," Lenok said. He was holding his staff with both hands. He didn't voice his thoughts, but he hadn't ever felt this much darkness in all his days.

Lightning flashed across the sky again, and they all saw dark figures standing around them, which faded when the flash was gone. Jon shot off a couple of shots forward. It was all very unsettling.

"No need for that," Lenok told him. "Your weapons will not stop them. They are not in the flesh."

"Then, what are they?"

"They are shadows. Seraphs fallen from the celestial Kingdom of Light. They cannot harm you either, but they can whisper. Beware their voices."

Nicolea moved up toward them as another spell of lightning filled the skies. He pointed toward a building. "If you look over there, there is movement coming out of the far corner."

Jon looked, and even looked into his binoculars,

trying to get a closer look. Sure enough, he noticed a larger fleshly motion coming from the corner in the darkness. After studying it a bit more, he confirmed that they were the giants he and Nicolea had come across on Serenity.

Soshiana had been using her scanner, trying to get a reading on the place. "I am detecting a human form in that building," she said.

"Phaleg?" Thermonte asked.

Lenok shook his head. "I don't think so."

Together they moved to the doors of the building and cautiously entered. Knowing that those shadows were all around them made them all feel uneasy. The light inside the building was only a fraction better than the light outside. Small indicator lights on equipment gave off a faint glow that allowed them to make out some of items in the room. Hanging from the ceiling, connected to many wires and tubes, was a female body, wrapped loosely in a black sheet. Her head moved and looked down at the group.

"How long you think she's been here?" Jon asked. "And what are they doing to her?"

Nicolea glanced at Lenok, who nodded back at him. They both knew then just who this woman was. It was

Lenok who told the others. "That is Queen Nathara, and she has been here a very long time. Her soul is all but gone, and her flesh is being kept alive. She is the mother of these giants, and these giants are the flesh being used to harbor the shadows."

"We've got to do something," Jon said.

Lenok put a hand on Jon's shoulder. "There is only one thing to do. Her life must end. Her soul is halfway in Hell now. She made her choice long ago, and they took her and made her what she is."

Jon looked over at Nicolea, who looked back at him. They both had the same look of disgust and pity on their face, but they knew it had to be done. "Everyone out," Jon ordered, as he and Nicolea both pulled out a heavy grenade, activating it with the thumb. Once everyone else was clear, they tossed the two grenades at what was left of that flesh.

The explosion was loud and bright, and the entire inside of the building lit up in fire before crumbling down upon itself. The blast threw Jon and Nicolea forward toward the center of the buildings.

The explosion drew the attention of the giants. The closer ones began to charge toward them. More could be seen coming from the distance, streaming from the strange mountains. Everyone on the team who carried a weapon used it. As giants fell, they could hear screams of anguish coming from their lips.

Soon, the giants seemed to strengthen and started to overcome them. Lenok stepped ahead of them, as their ammunition began to run low, and held his staff high.

"By the Lord of Light, I command you to return to your place in Hell." He struck the ground with the base of his staff, and a beam of bright light shot out of the top. The light was accompanied by a raging sound, like that of a large waterfall. As the light faded, the sound echoed until all was quiet.

The bodies of the giants had crumbled into dust, and as the lightning flashed again across the sky, no one seemed to see any shadowed figures. "Well," Jon said, blinking. "We could have used that a while back."

Lenok smiled. "There is a time and place for everything. Before wasn't the time, that moment was."

"A Prophet Warrior, huh?"

Lenok nodded. "It's what I do."

As they all began to settle their nerves, they heard a voice that seemed both far away and close. "Thermonte Electrik and company," the voice called out. It was the same voice that had identified itself as Doctor Phaleg over the comms inside the ship. "I am waiting for you. We need to talk, I think."

They all looked at the crime lord. He, in turn, looked back at each of them. Then he straightened his clothing and moved forward. "Come on," he said. "We have an invitation."

Together they moved toward the mountains, led now by Mr. Electrik.

CHAPTER ELEVEN

Alone

Doctor Phaleg stood at about six foot five. He was much taller than most of the humans there, but not nearly as tall as the giants that surrounded him. Mr. Electrik identified him as the doctor. They were on higher ground, looking through binoculars at the scene below.

"I don't see Jonah at all," stated Jon, looking for the assassin.

"My friend," Thermonte said, "he wouldn't look the same as you knew him, remember. I never saw him after I sent him here, only heard him. He kept his same voice."

"That much, I know." It was from Jon.

Nicolea peered up from his binoculars at the others. "So what's in the cave, I wonder?"

It was just at that moment that the doctor looked up and seemed to see the group on the hill. He smiled, then he spoke. "Don't be afraid. Regardless of what you've been told, I will not bite." He seemed to chuckle a bit at that old joke.

He seemed to be standing in a crater of some sort. At the rear of the crater was the cave they had been watching. Giant portable lights shone down on Doctor Phaleg and the giants as they worked. The giants were carrying boxes deeper into the cavern. Doctor Phaleg himself was dressed all in black, and his hair, slicked back, was black with touches of grey peppered all around.

Lightning continued to flash above, and the noise of the thunder rolled on. "Come on down, Thermonte, and bring your friends."

With that, they all knew they were found out. Too obvious. So one by one, they slowly made their way down to the crater where the doctor waited. Phaleg looked at each and every one of them. He tilted his head when he came to Lenok, dressed in his old robes, and smiled.

Coldly, he said, " I remember you."

Before Lenok could respond, Mr. Electrik jumped in front of them all and began confronting Phaleg. He seemed not to care who heard him, or what would happen to him. He was most definitely angry.

"You cut me out!" His voice was loud, not quite a shout. He had his forefinger pointing straight in Phaleg's face. "You promised me a part in this. I had to bring these people with me to come to the waters you told me about."

Again, Phaleg smiled. "And you have done exactly what we wanted you to do, my dear friend."

"And what was that?"

"You have brought them here to us. Here to Khair Din, where we needed them to be. Especially my old enemy, the one who might have stopped this operation, if only he were back in civilization."

Thermonte looked back at the group. Everyone seemed to know just who Phaleg was talking about. Lenok stepped up, supported by his staff. "Let me guess, this body was the first created, the purest." Lenok made a nod to Phaleg himself.

A wide grin stretched across Phaleg's face. "You are so smart, Lenok, son of Lesh. You have brought us to this situation. It is all your fault, Lenok. Have you not thought it would come to this?"

"What about me?" Thermonte shouted. "You just used me to bring them here!"

Phaleg placed a large hand on Thermonte's shoulder. "Andrelus," Phaleg called over his back, and a man walked up behind him.

"Andrelus," Phaleg said to him, "take our friend, Thermonte here, and show him his reward." Then, to Mr. Electrik, he said, "You will be a great leader."

"Of course, Doc," Andrelus said. He was a tall, lean, blond-haired man. But his eyes were still those of Jonah, the assassin Jon once chased across the galaxy. He smiled at Jon. "See you later, Agent Vega." Then he led Thermonte away, back into the cavern.

In automatic response, Jon, Nicolea, and Soshiana held up their weapons and pointed them toward Phaleg and Andrelus. Andrelus looked back, as did Mr. Electrik. Both smiled but kept walking. "I'm going to be the king," Thermonte shouted back. Andrelus just smiled.

"Your weapons are not going to work here," Phaleg told them. They all tested them and found that his words were true. The weapons did not fire.

Lenok stepped up, handing Nicolea his staff. "Keep this for me. I'm about to put a kink in his plans again."

Nicolea took it, looking over at Jon, who just looked confused as to what was going on. Soshiana stepped up between them. None of them could do a thing at the moment. Lenok stepped forward, and from the depths of his robe he pulled out a sword. Jon and Nicolea both wondered where that had come from. This old man was full of surprises.

If that wasn't strange enough, Phaleg then pulled a black sword out of nowhere. It looked more like a shadow of a sword, though that could have been a trick of the light. An extreme streak of lightning flashed across the sky, and when it was over, Lenok's blade was on fire.

To Jon, the battle that followed reminded him of something he had seen in films about ancient history. He could see each move clearly, almost as if they were moving in slow motion. They both seemed to know one another from the past. When the blades were brought together, it echoed within the crater they were in.

Every now and then one of the giants would walk over, but then move away when it saw Phaleg. Several other humans could be seen in the distance within the cave. Jon knew they were busy doing something and wanted desperately to see what was inside. He looked over at Nicolea, who knew what Jon was thinking.

He walked over to him. "You or me?"

"I'll go."

Nicolea nodded and watched his friend slowly make his way toward the cave. There were still-unknown objects all around the crater. All Jon had to do was to sneak up to the entrance, while hiding from the eyes of Phaleg. He was hoping that Phaleg was keeping his eyes on Lenok, not himself as he was moving ahead.

Lightning continued to crack open the skies as Jon finally moved into the entrance of the cave itself. Once inside, and after moving a little deeper, he saw what was there. It was the same thing he and Nicolea had seen on Serenity, and it was active. Strange lights lit up the device, which looked like the one on Serenity. This time, instead of a portal of water, Jon saw yellow lights shining just within the entrance of the portal. Where this portal led, he didn't know. He just knew he had to take it out and destroy it completely.

Moving extremely slowly, and whispering into the mic attached to his headgear so the others knew what was going on, he made his way to attach explosives around the device. By now, however, most of the giants and humans had already gone through it. He knew they would have to go fight this enemy elsewhere also.

Outside the cave entrance, Lenok seemed to be losing the battle. It was hard for him to fight this big man with these ancient swords. Nicolea knew just how old Lenok actually was. He knew he couldn't hold out for long. He wasn't quite sure about this Phaleg, and just how they had met before, but he had a good idea. He had read the scrolls. These creatures had been a part of his life in some way. Then he wondered if he himself would be a part of this darkness, seduced by these shadows and their whispers.

He was about to move when Soshiana stopped him. She nodded past him. He turned to look, seeing Jon returning from the cavern. When Jon was close enough, he tossed the detonator to Nicolea, who then stepped forward.

"Phaleg!" Nicolea shouted at the strange man.

The fight stopped, and the doctor turned to see Nicolea. "What do you want?"

Nicolea held up the detonator. "You're about to miss your jump," he said, and he detonated the explosives within the cave.

A multicolored fire burst from the cavern's entrance, and the cave itself collapsed. Phaleg's eyes grew wide, and his face showed a mixture of surprise, anger, and hate. He turned with his sword and sliced at Lenok, who took the hit with his chest and fell onto his back. Lenok's sword quit burning as he dropped it, and it landed with a thud.

Jon charged Phaleg, but with a backhand he smacked Jon several feet back onto the ground. Jon felt blood coming from his chin and mouth where he had been hit. Soshiana grabbed a knife from her belt and charged. Her blade penetrated Phaleg's shoulder, but he threw her off quickly.

Phaleg removed a device from his own belt and pressed one of the buttons on it. "There is one thing you forget. Surely Mr. Electrik told you that I built the FTL ship you all came in. Now there is no FTL drive to get you back."

Soshiana looked up with her long-range field glasses and watched the FTL engines detach from the ship and float away from it, slowly moving into the atmosphere of the planet.

During this exchange Lenok had moved and once again grabbed his sword. He now threw it at Phaleg, and the blade stuck deep in his chest. Jon watched as the shadowed blade vanished back into the shadows.

Nicolea moved closer to Lenok, and the sword burst into flames once again, burning the flesh from Phaleg. Phaleg never screamed in pain. He looked at the others. "This doesn't matter. I have control of your world now."

One final small puff of flame surrounded Phaleg, and he was gone. The oxygen bubble that kept them all safe was gone, and they had to hurry and replace their face masks.

Lenok refused his mask. He spoke instead to Nicolea and Jon, and Soshiana stood behind them listening to it all. "They need you back quick. Return to Bel Terra and Illosha. There you will learn what you must do. My time is here, and now I get to go through the waters."

He glanced up past them and looked at Soshiana. He said, "There is always hope for you." Then Lenok died.

Soshiana was taken aback by this. It was like he was looking into her soul. They all stood up, and in the distance, they saw a shadowed figure wavering in the wind.

"You will not make it back in time," said the figure. "And you will lose."

Nicolea started to lead the others toward where they had left the shuttle, occasionally looking back at the dark figure. He knew it was the Dark Seraph. Soon they had gotten onto the shuttle and were heading back to the FTL ship.

Once inside, they followed Soshiana to the small bridge, where they all noticed that the water in space was no longer there.

"What happened to it?" Jon asked.

"We will never know, perhaps," answered Nicolea. He watched Soshiana fiddle with the controls.

She must have known he was watching, for she spoke on cue. "The FTL engines and drives have been destroyed, but we still have light speed. Just not sure about the fuel. I'm heading back on the coordinate path we came up here on. While you two sleep in the pods, I'll maintain direction toward home."

Nicolea came over to her. "What's wrong?"

She came out with it. She didn't usually show emotion, but now her anger and sadness were obvious. "All those years I worked for him, was loyal to him, and he just left me behind. And then there was that priest guy. How did he know my programming, and just how to rewrite it with his words?"

"Lenok reprogrammed you?"

"He must have. Something feels…different." Soshiana looked uncertain, an uncommon feeling for her.

"Do you remember your life before you became a bio-tek?"

"I think so," she said. "But I don't know if it is real or programming. You know they took me when I was dying."

"You get us home, and I will do some research to see how you lived before you became a bio-tek." Nicolea then said, "What he said about hope, perhaps he was referring to your memories. You are more human than you think. No matter what you do to your body, how you live your life, or what you have done, you can always let the Lord of Light into your heart."

"What if my heart is a machine?" she asked. She looked at him then.

Nicolea smiled. "I don't think it is, after seeing your expressions today."

She gave a quick smile, then turned back to her work. Nicolea turned to see Jon rubbing the back of his neck. "You okay?" Nicolea asked Jon, as he moved toward him and the bridge doorway. Sitting next to the door was the staff Lenok had handed to him. He grabbed it.

"I'm going to go grab a shower," he replied. "Then something to eat before we go back into the sleeping pods."

"Let's stay up a week or two before going down," Nicolea suggested. "We have time."

Jon nodded in agreement. "Sure," he said. "I could do some exercises, get back in shape. I haven't done that in two years."

Both smiled. Nicolea saw that Mr. Electrik was no longer in Jon's thoughts. He didn't know why, but he was thankful for it. "I'm going to go read before we eat. Let me know when you are ready," he said, and he and Jon left the bridge.

Soshiana looked to be deep in thought as she watched the instruments. She had a lot of thinking to do, and she had the time for it now.

CHAPTER TWELVE
Third Scroll of Dan

Nicolea stepped into the room Lenok had used on the way to the planet. He would of course have to sleep for most of the journey. For now, though, he would eat, shower, have conversations with Jon and Soshiana, and generally enjoy some leisure before going down. It would be good to be normal for a time. But first, he was going to read. He pulled out a scroll from the satchel Lenok had left for him, and began to read.

It was near the end of the first journey of Lenok, son of Lesh, as a Prophet Warrior. He only had one more task he needed to complete before returning to the Isle of Illosha. Lenok had just left the Ash Mountains and was taking a rest near the Grey Lake in Sandylyn Plains when the White Seraph walked up to him, calling him by name.

"Lenok, you must travel to Machonon, to the oasis known as Lamash just within the land. It rests on the Grey River leading south, but you will not take that river. You will go the way of the Bitter Pass, to the east of the Grey Lake, and come in from the north in the sands."

Lenok just nodded in agreement. The Lord of Light had never let him down in any way, and he was sure this would be the best route, even though the most direct route was down the river.

The White Seraph continued to speak. "You must speak to the son of Kief Dan, who is now protected by the Lord of Light. He has two sons. You will place a mark of red onto the forehead of one of the sons; on the other son's forehead you will place a mark of wet mud from the river. You must tell Jerod that his sons will be the fathers of two kingdoms. One kingdom will follow the ways of their grandfather, Kief Dan. The other will be established in the ways of the Lord of Light. One of his descendants will follow the path of a Prophet Warrior. Tell him none of this will come to pass in his time, or in his son's lifetimes."

"Which mark will follow God?" asked Lenok. It was simply curiosity.

"That is not anyone's concern, but His." Then the White Seraph turned and walked back into the wind.

Lenok gathered up his belongings and headed east toward the Bitter Pass. It was called the Bitter Pass because of the soured scent that came up from an underground lake beneath the land. As he crossed into the territory, he met a family of four moving north, and they told him they were heading to New Galmesh, in the land of Aurora.

Fourteen days later, Lenok had passed into the desert, where he began heading south. He came to the downhill path leading straight into the oasis near the river a few days later. He entered the township on the twenty-first day of his journey and immediately began looking for Jerod.

Lenok soon saw a man that he recognized, even though he had never before seen him. He walked up to him, leaning on his staff. "Jerod Dan," he said, and Jerod looked at him with curiosity.

Lenok introduced himself. "I am a Prophet Warrior, sent by the Lord of Light to bring comfort to you. You have two sons, which I must mark for the Lord. But first, I must gather mud from the river."

Jerod believed and escorted the Prophet Warrior to the river's edge and to his home, where his wife, Lynla, was feeding the twins. This was something Lenok had not expected.

Lenok removed a red dye from his bag and set that on the table near the children, who were not yet a year old. Mixing the mud and setting a bit near the dye, Lenok knelt and prayed in front of the children. Then he stood up and marked one child with the red dye and the other with the mud. Then he turned to Jerod and told him what the White Seraph had told him.

He said, "Your sons will be the fathers of two kingdoms. One kingdom will follow the ways of your father, Kief Dan. The other will be established in the ways of the Lord of Light. One descendant will follow the path of a Prophet Warrior. This will not happen in your lifetime, nor your son's lifetimes. Your seed will flourish through your sons."

Then Jerod and his wife praised the Lord of Light and gave thanks. They asked Lenok to remain and share the evening meal with them, which he happily did. Afterward he expressed his thanks and made ready to leave, but before he could do so, pirates attacked from the river. Panicked screams could be heard outside, and immediately Lenok grabbed his staff and headed out.

He freed those who were being captured, knocking the pirates out of his way with his staff. The rest of the pirates left their small river ship and came to the aid of their friends on land. Arrows shot at Lenok were missing their mark, and swinging swords were being rebuffed by hard knocks to bodies from Lenok's staff. Lenok fought well, but there were far more pirates than one man could be expected to overcome, and he began to lose ground.

Then just when it appeared that the pirates would overtake him, Lenok held the staff high and shouted, "Enough!"

Shards of lightning shot from his staff and pierced every pirate. Their bodies hollowed out and burned to dust. Then Lenok heard a whisper in his ear. It was the voice of the White Seraph. "Get on the river ship, and you will be taken upriver all the way to Northshire. It is time to return."

Lenok stepped onto the river ship, and the winds blew north, back up the river, and Lenok returned to the Isle of Illosha.

Nicolea placed the scroll he had been reading back into the satchel. After reading through many scrolls, especially those concerning his ancestors, he was beginning to understand things more. Like everything else, his past had good and evil. He just thanked the Lord of Light that he was able to understand.

It had been three weeks since Lenok's death on the shadowed world, and Nicolea was about to go down to sleep in his pod when Soshiana walked into his room. "Can I ask you something?"

He nodded. "Sure."

"Do you think there is a chance I do still have a soul, as you call it?"

Nicolea thought for just a moment. "You had loyalty to Thermonte Electrik for many many years, did you not?"

"Twelve years," she replied.

"And in those twelve years, you have been a loyal member of his family, no matter what he did or said." She nodded. "And you were hurt, when he betrayed us down on the planet and took Phaleg's side?"

"I felt something. Surprise or anger." She stumbled. "I don't know. It did hurt whatever it was."

"Then I believe you do still have a soul. Listening to you talk now, I believe it," he told her. "There is no such thing as a *true* artificial intelligence anyway, because there is always a man or woman behind the A.I. programming it. Even if there were, though, you don't act like one anymore."

Soshiana just stood there. "I don't sleep or eat. How can I be human?"

"Because Doctor Phaleg could alter the flesh, but not the spirit and soul."

After a minute, she returned a little bit of a smile. "I don't think Agent Vega likes me very much."

"People can change."

Then she helped him into the sleeping pod they had

moved into his room, and he fell into a deep sleep. Soshiana made her way back to the bridge to check on navigation. She pondered Nicolea's words. Lately she had spent much time thinking about him, Lenok, this Lord they believed in, and where she fit into it all. Undoubtedly, she would have more questions for Nicolea when he woke.

CHAPTER THIRTEEN

Dust

The winds stirred the earth as they blew. Walking through the desert, the unknown man headed toward the town of Dust, which was named after the colony world of Dust. The town of Dust had been in existence for nearly thirty years and was a booming town. It was also a rough town, and men openly carried hand held weapons on their person. Life was tough there. There was mining in the Sharai Mountains, in which Dust was nestled on three sides. Panning for gold in the river was popular with newcomers to the town. The gold was used in the local saloons and brothels.

As the unknown man made his way into the town, with the wind still stirring up the dirt around him, he was greeted by many drunken women trying to sell him their services. He looked around and watched the inhabitants of the town, who all seemed drunk.

It was morning, and the sun had been up for several hours now. The local law was a sheriff named Bolen. He saw the stranger, whose face was covered with a dirty brown handkerchief. In fact, everything he was wearing was a murky brown, except for his black boots and a loose-fitting shirt. The vest he wore was that dirty brown as was the worn, wide-brimmed hat on his head.

Sheriff Bolen walked out into the middle of the dirty street and walked toward the new man. "Can I help you?" On his hip was an old blaster pistol he had gotten many years ago.

The unknown man carried no known weapons. None that Bolen could see. "Mister, I asked you a question."

"I heard you," the man replied. "Do you approve of the evil going on in this town?"

The sheriff chuckled. "This is just life here," he said. "We're a colony, and we make our own laws. The rest of the galaxy has no jurisdiction here."

The unknown man looked around. "I'm looking for a righteous man."

"You're in the wrong town, Mister," the sheriff

chuckled. Looking around, the sheriff noticed others watching his transaction with this man. The unknown man had also noticed. The sheriff said, "Listen, partner, where is your ship? Nothing has landed at the spaceport in several days.

The unknown man just looked at him. There was something about the stranger's eyes; it was the way he looked at him. The sheriff began to get nervous. This man didn't seem right. He never answered him, but just stood there looking at Sheriff Bolen.

"I don't know any righteous man," he finally said to the man. "Do you know for sure he is here?"

The man looked up over the sheriff's head, looking around the town. "He is here." Then a moment of strange silence, before he spoke again. "This town contains so much evil. You need to deal with it, Sheriff."

Bolen breathed in. "I didn't catch your name."

Nothing.

Bolen spoke again. "You can check the registry at the spaceport for your righteous man. Then you need to get out. We don't want your kind here. You understand, Mister?"

Just then, a drunken woman strolled out of the saloon and saw the sheriff. "Hey Sheriff!" she called out.

"Those guys are at it again!"

"I'll be right there, Marta," he called back. Then to the man, he said, "I hope you're planning to follow our laws. Don't do anything that will cause me to hunt you down. Me and my deputies will be keeping our eyes on you, and you won't know who they are."

Then after another look into those strange, old eyes, Sheriff Bolen turned and followed the woman as she went back into the saloon.

Toward the base of the mountains there sat several houses. They had been there for years, worn and in different stages of decay. However, there was one of the houses further back that looked much newer. Jesse Boone lived there with his wife, Abagael, and his daughter Maggie. Maggie was twelve years old, but they had all lived there for just four years. Jesse worked as a miner up in the hills near the river valley. He wasn't well-liked in the town, for he didn't live like the rest of the township.

This was the house the unknown man began walking to. The man knew there were eyes upon him, and that there would be much grief for his choice of destination. There was, in fact, one man, one of the drunkards, that slowly stood up. He watched the unknown man move toward Jesse Boone's house. He, himself, moved as quick as he could, and made his way across the street and into the saloon. One man was dead on the floor, and one close to death was slumped in a chair. Sheriff Bolen stood at the bar with a drink in his hand.

The drunkard's name was Hossa. He made his way near the sheriff. Bolen took a drink and turned around. "That stranger made his way straight to Jesse Boone's house, Sheriff."

Bolen remembered who the man was looking for: a righteous man. "What's that got to do with me, Hossa?"

"Maybe this stranger is the law, I mean, maybe the real law."

The sheriff looked at him sternly and considered backhanding him for a moment. Hossa continued. "I don't mean to say you ain't the law, sheriff, I'm just saying...you know, the galaxy law."

Sheriff Bolen knew what the drunken man was talking about. The stranger hadn't answered his questions, or even given him his name. He finished off his drink and turned around. In the saloon, there were many people, many of them worked for Bolen. "Okay, boys," he shouted across the room. "Gather the others, we gonna find out what this stranger is up to. Maybe we can turn him over to the Empire for some cash."

Meanwhile, the unknown man had knocked on the Boone door. Jesse opened the door. The man spoke quickly and first. "Are you Jesse Boone?"

Jesse nodded that he was. "Yes."

The man stepped through the door and closed it behind him, moving Jesse back a bit. His wife came from around the corner to see who their visitor was. "I am Gideon. You are to leave this town and head north to where an oasis of green waits for you."

Jesse had never seen this man before, but he instantly knew that he was to be obeyed. Jesse and his family were followers of the Lord of Light, which had been made illegal by the new Empire that had formed nearly four years ago. Dust was not a friendly town, it was a place people of criminal tendencies went to hide. That meant it was also a good place for Jesse and his family to hide.

After hearing the man's words, Jesse and his family began to quickly gather the essentials in bags. "Are you coming with us?" he asked the man.

"I will make sure that you safely depart," said Gideon, "but I have work here in Dust."

Jesse looked into the man's eyes. They were old, ancient, and Jesse knew those eyes had seen much. He would never know just how much Gideon had seen.

Soon there was a knock on the door. It was the sheriff. "Jesse Boone, this is Sheriff Bolen. Send us the stranger, or you will face the mob."

Jesse took a glance out the window. Not only was it the sheriff, but it looked as if every disreputable member of society was there as well. In Dust that was quite a large number. His wife and daughter came back into the room after getting everything together they would need for the journey north.

Then Gideon said to them, "Regardless of what you hear or see after you leave, do not feel grief. This town is evil, and this town must be dealt with. Trust the Light of the Lord to guide you."

The knock on the door had gotten stronger and louder. Jesse took his family and headed out the back door. The man reached out and opened the front door after he was sure the family had gotten out safely. He looked up and around above the townsfolk's heads as if breathing in the air around them. He knew, then, that the Boone family had not been followed.

Put out, the sheriff grabbed the man by his vest and flung him to the ground. He then kicked him several times until Gideon was lying in the dusty street. Finally,

Sheriff Bolen asked, "Who are you, Mister? You tell us now. Are you with the Empire?"

The man wiped the blood from a small cut on his face. "Your Empire means nothing," was his only answer. Slowly, he began to stand up. "There is evil in this town of Dust, and to dust, this town will return."

Everyone laughed, even the sheriff. He pulled his blaster pistol from the holster hanging at his side. "And what does that mean, Mister? I tell you what it means. It means you got no idea who you're dealing with. We could just kill you, or maybe we should just hand you over to the Empire. Is there a reward?"

The man reached up inside his left sleeve and pulled out a silver rod with his right hand. He shook his right hand, and the rod grew into a silver staff. The crowd of townsfolk were somewhat taken aback, but the sheriff extended his gun outward, pointing it at the man's chest. "What are you doing?" Bolen demanded to know.

"This is the Staff of the Lord of Light given to me to destroy this town of sin and evil. Darkness reigns here, and it will end. I am Gideon, the destroyer of evil, sent by the One True God, the Lord of Light, to turn this town back to dust."

Sheriff Bolen fired his weapon at the man. Somehow,

he missed. Gideon raised the staff up high, and brought it down, straight and hard, to the ground.

Jesse and his family had reached the second tier of the mountain. A path there led deeper into the mountain valley behind. Just as his wife and daughter had stepped over onto the trail, they heard a loud, deafening boom. Abagael grabbed Maggie and fell forward onto the path, thinking it would protect her. Jesse jumped onto the path and turned around, waiting for a fight. He thought maybe someone had followed them. Instead, he saw a rising cloud of dust.

A moment later dust and wind rushed by him, settling farther along the path. Some of it settled on his wife as she lay on the path holding Maggie. Jesse never saw what had actually happened to Dust, and never went back to find out.

From the cloud of lingering dust surrounding the town, a single man walked out into the desert lands. He was once again an unknown man, a man no one knew. He would be called back, one day.

Author's Note

This is the second edition of the first book in the World of Strangers and Pilgrims Series. This edition has been revised and updated to include a better understanding of the story. Into Shadow' Fire, the second book in the series, will be updated soon and re-released in a second edition. Look forward for the third installment, Shadow's Winter, coming out soon.

Thanks for everyone who have enjoyed reading my books, and will continue to support me by reading those books I have yet to write. I am always interested in hearing from my readers. Any comments made are always a helpful tool for me.

This is a Christian Science Fiction book, and you will find some Biblically-inspired stories within the larger tale. As some of our characters will find, there is always hope. No matter your walk in life, there is hope for you, too. Below I have put in the Romans Road to Salvation to help. I would suggest you go to your local church and talk to someone there about salvation.

The greatest road anyone will ever travel: The Romans Road of Salvation

Romans 3:23 KJV "For all have sinned, and come short of the glory of God;"

Romans 6:23 KJV "For the wages of sin *is* death; but the gift of God *is* eternal life through Jesus Christ our Lord."

Romans 5:8 KJV "But God commendeth his love toward us, in that, while we were yet sinners, Christ died for us."

Romans 10:9 KJV "That if thou shalt confess with thy mouth the Lord Jesus, and shalt believe in thine heart that God hath raised him from the dead, thou shalt be saved."

Romans 10:13 KJV "For whosoever shall call upon the name of the Lord shall be saved."

Romans 8:1 KJV "*There is* therefore now no

condemnation to them which are in Christ Jesus, who walk not after the flesh, but after the Spirit."

Romans 8:38-39 KJV "For I am persuaded, that neither death, nor life, nor angels, nor principalities, nor powers, nor things present, nor things to come, nor height, nor depth, nor any other creature, shall be able to separate us from the love of God, which is in Christ Jesus our Lord."

ABOUT THE AUTHOR

Mark Castleberry has been a fan of science fiction and fantasy fan since childhood. He grew up on a lake in Alabama, wanting to write since high school. All the characters and stories have been lodged in his head for many years and writing them down for most of his life never having anything published, until the Internet opened up and self-publishing became an option. Now he resides in Missouri with his wife and two cats. He now writes a very imaginatively, fast-paced series of books and stories with Christian influences that just may leave you breathless. His books contain Christian morals and values, and the tales weaved into it come from the Bible.

In addition to writing books and stories for the young adult audience, he runs the Stranger and Pilgrims Podcast, which host old time radio stories and audio dramas that can open up your imagination. You can follow the author on several social media sites as well as his website at www.strangerspilgrims.com

EDITORIAL REVIEW

Mark Castleberry's Conflict with Shadows is a fascinating tale about the adventures of Jon Vega and Nicholea Dan in their pursuit to stop the Darkness from destroying their world. The peaceful planet of Serenity was suddenly being attacked by an unknown enemy. This planet was unclaimed by both the Republic alliance and the Federation governments. The two factions were still not on good terms because of the unitary split from several decades ago, but neither one of the factions was the cause of the sudden violence that was currently taking place in Serenity. It came as a shock to both sides when they heard news of the attack and that several of their people were injured and dead. After making sure both sides were innocent, the President of the Republic and the Prime Minister of the Federation decided to set aside their differences and work together to stop the destruction from spreading further. After seeing the damage that the unknown enemy did to Serenity, Jon Vega, the best agent of the republic, and Nicholea Dan, the best protector of the Federation, were both sent to infiltrate the enemy's base in Serenity to investigate further. Little did they know that this was more than just a simple attack; this was the start of their journey to save their world and the souls of mankind.

This book is so engrossing, it easily drew me into the plot. Conflict with Shadows: The World of Strangers and Pilgrims Book 1 by Mark Castleberry is a fast-paced book I surely didn't want to miss. The story was so captivating that I read the book continuously in an effort to quickly find out what happened next. The story was filled with a lot of interesting and thrilling action scenes that constantly had me on the edge of my seat. Aside from the great plot, the story is also filled with valuable lessons, like having faith during the toughest of times, which makes it even more worth the read. The science fiction element of this book is so gripping that I can't get it out of my mind. It truly is a well-written piece and I feel lucky to have come across such a marvelous book. An astonishing, notable work.

Reviewed by Jessica Barbosa for Readers' Favorite
5 Star Review

<u>Also By The Author</u>:

THE WAY OF CAIN AND JONAH'S RUN

<u>THE WORLD OF STRANGERS AND PILGRIMS SERIES</u>

1. CONFLICT WITH SHADOWS
2. INTO SHADOW'S FIRE
3. SHADOW'S WINTER

Published by Strangers and Pilgrims Publishing
www.strangerspilgrims.com